DARK LEGION

Miss Renae

Copyright © 2023 by Miss Renae

All rights reserved.

No part of this publication may be reproduced, distributed, or transmitted in any form or by any means, including photocopying, recording, or other electronic or mechanical methods, without the prior written permission of the publisher, except as permitted by U.S. copyright law. For permission requests, contact [include publisher/author contact info].

The story, all names, characters, and incidents portrayed in this production are fictitious. No identification with actual persons (living or deceased), places, buildings, and products is intended or should be inferred.

Book Cover by Osiya

Editor Scarlett Chase

GET HELP

If you or a loved one need help, always reach out! These are some amazing resources. Protect your mental health. Remember, you're **NOT** alone.

National Suicide Prevention Lifeline 800 273-TALK **National Suicide Hotline** 800 784-243 **Domestic Violence and Intimate Partner Violence** 800 799-7233 **Sexual Assault** 800 656-4673

AUTHOR'S NOTE

A Paranormal Why Choose Romance, meaning the main character does not have to choose between her love interests. This is a slow burn. FMC only falls for one of her guys in book one.

This book contains Trigger Warnings. Reader's discretion is advised.

This book contains 18 plus content, including adult-n@pping, gore, sexual content, DA, and dark humor.

If any of the above mention is triggering, please skip this book. Mental health is very important. Let's not yuck anyone else's yum.

DEDICATION

This book wouldn't have been possible without my amazing Alpha readers. Bobby, Nikki, and Chardonae.

Thank you so much for sticking by my side as I worked through writer's block and developed the Dark Legion MC.

These amazing ladies helped choose names, locations, and story details.

Bobby's favorite duo is Steele and Snake. Those two are the definition of double trouble. Nikki loves our daddy-dom Scar. We may be fighting for him! Chardonae adores our cinnamon roll Nate and our overprotective shifter Tank.

We hope you love them too.

Chapter 1

KATRINA

It's been five days since we left. Five days since I packed us into this car and fled in the middle of the night. The sun began to rise and Leona was passed out in her car seat, completely oblivious to the dangers we would be in if he found us.

He can't ever find us. If he did, I'm as good as dead and my daughter? NO.

I shook my head at those thoughts. I couldn't let myself imagine, not even for a second, what could have happened to my sweet and innocent little girl.

Up ahead was the only service station for many miles. I didn't have a choice but to stop. As I pulled into the mostly empty station, I debated if I should wake Leona but decided I'd rather have her fussy than let her out of my sight.

"Baby," I whispered. She scrunched her nose adorably before her eyelids fluttered open. "Are you hungry? Let's get something to eat."

I gave her a small smile. Her bright blue eyes searched around frantically. My heart squeezed at the fear I saw. Fear he put there. My eyes stung with unshed tears as I unbuckled her from her booster seat.

"Where is daddy?" Her tiny voice was unsure and groggy from sleep.

"He's not here, baby. Let's get donuts."

I took her hand, and we walked inside the station. The bell overhead rang as it closed. Leona let my hand go, and took off toward the wall of sugary treats. Just that small distance sent a wave of anxiety through me. I quickly grabbed a hot coffee and juice box, not wanting to be separated from her for too long. I slammed into a hard chest, and my coffee instantly covered us both.

"I'm so sorry. I should have been watching where I was going."

I grabbed napkins and tried to dry off his white t-shirt in a haste to fix the damage I'd already caused. My anxiety made each inhale painful. His hand gripped my wrist to stop me from embarrassing myself further.

"It's fine, dove."

I flinched at the contact, so used to pain-filled touches that when his giant hands caressed mine, I found myself lost in his honey eyes. I gasped in surprise and glanced back down at his biker boots. Fearful of pissing him off, I murmured another apology.

A low growl came from the man in front of me, the sound threatening and deadly. I whimpered and attempted to take a step back, but my hip rammed into the countertop of the coffee bar. My husband had conditioned me over the years to never make eye contact with anyone or there would be consequences.

"I-I'm so sorry," I breathed as I backed away from him further, and rubbed my hip softly. The bruises along my side made the impact more painful.

"Mama, look! I got you one with sprinkles."

Leona's blonde curls came into view. My throat felt like a frog was stuck, afraid if I spoke, my voice would shake again. So instead, I just gave her a smile and kissed the top of her head. Leona bounced all the way to the front in excitement and set our donuts on the counter. I began rummaging around for my wallet. After checking it a few times, I realized my wallet was missing.

"I'm sorry. I left my wallet in the car. We will be right back."

The cashier gave me an annoyed look. His jaw was rigid with irritation. I pulled Leona to my side and shuffled toward the door. The same man I bumped into moments before was leaning against the wall, watching me. I felt trapped and my heart drummed wildly with uncertainty. His caramel eyes met mine, and all I saw was genuine kindness shining back in their depths.

"Paul, put the lady's items on my tab," he said, never taking his eyes off mine.

I should've protested that this biker was helping me. I've learned that anytime someone does something kind, they always want something in return. The stranger's eyes flicked to Leona briefly.

Hell no.

I pulled her slightly behind me and gave him my best glare. His nostrils flared. A slight curve crossed his lips that pulled at the scars along his jaw and cheeks.

"Paul, add a coffee, too. I spilt mama bear's last one."

At the reminder, my eyes darted down to his still damp t-shirt, a reminder mine was also wet.

Great, now I'll need to change soon.

The weather was too cold to walk around in wet clothes.

"You got it, boss," he responded.

"Mama," Leona said as she tugged on the hem of my shirt. "Can I eat my donut now?"

"Oh yeah, sure baby."

She ran back to the counter, grabbed our bag, and picked up my coffee. She was sweet for trying to carry it. However, the last thing I needed was to spill yet another coffee in this store.

I stopped by the exit and found the courage to look into his honey eyes again. This close, I could see the left eye was slightly darker than the right and jagged lines marred his handsome face. It didn't take away from how handsome he was, but added to it. I could get lost in those eyes.

"Thank you for the coffee, and I'm so sorry about your shirt," I practically whispered. Somehow he heard me and the smile he gave me was breathtaking.

"It's my pleasure."

The deep gravel in his voice made me blush. I dipped my head to hide my reaction to him.

What is wrong with me?

No man had ever had this kind of effect on me before.

"Thank you for the donut," Leona chirped with a mouthful of food.

"You're quite welcome, little bird." He looked back at me. "Never apologize to me again."

"I didn't mean–" His growl cut me off from finishing yet another apology. His dark brow raised slightly, a dare to defy him.

"Dove. Do. Not. Apologize," he emphasized each word.

I felt the need to look away and my eyes landed on a patch on his leather jacket. An intricate wolf and rose next to the word President.

Is he in a gang?

I licked my lips as I shifted from foot to foot before I felt brave enough to look at him again. I gave him a small nod, which he returned.

"Mama, I'm cold," Leona complained, and broke our stare off.

"Okay baby, let's go get you warm."

The door chimed as the stranger stepped out the door. The sound of motorcycles roared to life before we even had left the store. I wished to get one last glance at the mystery stranger. I pushed out the door and my eyes darted around the now empty parking lot. I didn't really know why, but I felt disappointed he was already gone.

I didn't even get his name.

I buckled Leona into the seat, and I gave her my donut as well, not feeling up to eating anything. I searched for my wallet. Not under the seat, not in the center console. It's then I realized my wallet was gone. I must have dropped it at our last stop.

"Fuck!" I screamed out and slammed the trunk closed.

I willed the tears not to fall and rested my forehead on the cool metal of the car to calm myself.

What are we going to do? I have maybe seven dollars in change.

A sob racked my body, one that I tried to silence by covering my mouth.

"What's the matter?"

I startled and looked around for the man who spoke as I wished it was the handsome stranger from inside.

"A pretty little thing like you shouldn't be hanging around these parts by yourself. Even if it is morning. It's just not safe."

He stepped closer as he spoke, almost like he was cornering his prey. The man was tall and lanky, but at my height, anyone was tall by comparison. He wore a leather jacket with a cobra and knife symbol.

"We are just leaving," I answered as I lifted my chin in false bravado. One I had mastered over the years.

"We?" he questioned. His head tilted slightly as he studied me, and a grin spread across his face.

Fuck me! Why are you so stupid, Katrina?

He mirrored every step I took toward the driver's door. A feral glint in his eyes that sent a shiver of fear down my spine.

"Please," I begged and held a shaky hand up.

I now stood in front of Leona's door, too afraid to move. He could easily grab her if I didn't start the engine fast enough. Gravel crunched from behind me, but I didn't dare take my eyes off the man before me. Somehow, I knew he was the bigger threat.

"I love it when they beg," a voice said from behind me. My back stiffened as I contemplated my next move.

The man before me inhaled deeply before he let out a groan as he licked his lips. The movement was predatory. His gaze dipped down my body, still covered in wet coffee, the thin fabric not leaving much up to the imagination. I suppressed the urge to cover myself. I couldn't show weakness. Within a blink, the man in front of me had my back pinned against the car. His hand encased my throat, his eyes hypnotized mine.

How did he move so fast? It's not possible.

"Mama!" Leona screamed and pounded on the window behind me, but those eyes held me captive. I couldn't pull my gaze from him, no matter how much I tried.

"You will not run, will you, my pet? You're going to do as I say, aren't you?" he asked in a velvet like voice, one that lulled me into submission.

My erratic heart slowed at his words while my brain urged me to fight. A tingling sensation settled over my fingers and toes, and my brain felt sluggish.

"Stop playing with your food, Spider."

Being called food should have got my ass into gear, but still I was frozen. A single tear ran down my cheek as I fought for control of my body.

What is happening to me?

"Please don't hurt my daughter. Take whatever you want."

The only thing I cared about was my little girl. I didn't escape one monster, only to be thrown into the arms of another. Both men bursted out with laughter and made me flinch. The one holding me against the car, Spider, ran a hand down my body and groped my hips. I hissed in pain. The last time John took his pleasures from my body, he was extremely rough and the bruises he left behind still hadn't healed.

"Pet. Pet. Pet. You can not offer me anything that isn't already mine to take. I am your master and as long as you behave, I'll spare your child. For now."

A malicious smile crossed his ugly face that revealed teeth that seem too large for his face. Before I had time to respond, the roar of motorcycles' engines in the distance was coming in fast.

"Fuck! Let's go! We can't be here when the Dark Legion MC shows up," the other guy said frantically.

God damn it! How many motorcycle gangs are in this stupid town?

Spider, my current "master", growled in frustration, clearly not liking his game being interrupted. His fingers dug into my neck tighter and stole the air from my lungs. I finally found the strength to fight back. My nails dug into his forearms in an attempt to free myself, but his strength overpowered mine and no matter how hard I fought, I couldn't escape him.

"Spider!" he bellowed again. "Fine! Take the girl and meet me at the clubhouse."

Spider scooped me up into his arms like I weighed nothing and took off into the trees surrounding the service station. I screamed and kicked, but it was no use. I couldn't break free of his hold. The trees sped past us in a blur of colors, too fast for my eyes to track.

"Leona, RUN!" I screamed one last time as a prick on my

shoulder had my vision blurring and white hot pain erupted down my body.

What did he stab me with? No! If he gets me to a secondary location, that's it.

I tried to fight again, but my limbs wouldn't respond. My sluggish brain could barely comprehend what was happening as I fell to the ground, my clothing instantly wet from the icy puddles.

What did Spider give me?

I wiped my shoulder where the needle pierced my skin. My fingers came back coated in a sticky crimson. Blood.

What the hell? Why would I be bleeding from a needle?

I squinted, trying to identify my surroundings, and Spider's face came into view, his mouth covered in crimson.

Did he bite me?

I cried out in fear as my body tried to catch up with my brain, but it was no use. Whatever coursed through my body had taken control of my reflexes. The burning pain in my shoulder only got worse.

"Be a good little pet and stay put until I return for you."

The need to obey him overwhelmed me. The fight to escape left my body almost instantly. Fading in and out of consciousness, I was startled awake by a loud bang. My eyes burned like sandpaper as I tried and failed to see what was going on around me.

"Where is she?" a demanding voice boomed, followed by a chorus of low and menacing growls.

What is that?

A shiver of fear rolled down my spine. My erratic heartbeat brought another wave of nausea before my vision tunneled and pulled me into the abyss.

Chapter 2
SCAR

Leaving the dark-haired beauty inside the gas station put me on edge. I didn't understand why. Any woman and child entering the Dark Legion territory were safe.

So why do I feel that leaving them alone was a mistake?

I was supposed to be checking in with Reap and getting a status update on our next run, but all I could think about was the fear that haunted her electric-blue eyes. Desperation clouded by a darkness that called to my soul.

"Pres? What's going on?" my brother questioned, interrupting my thoughts.

I rubbed a hand down my face, then gave him my full attention. Thick onyx hair hung over dark brown eyes. Eyes like the beautiful, carefree girl we lost all those years ago. Plagued by those memories every time I closed my eyes. A reel of nightmares that were in a never-ending cycle. A reminder of all the ways I'd failed her.

"While making my rounds, I stopped at the service station up the road. This woman and her child were just passing through. Something about her just isn't sitting right with me."

Tank's brows furrowed as he listened. The protector in him pushed him to his feet.

"You left them alone?" he growled, as he slung on his cut and headed toward the door.

"Are you questioning if they would be safe in my territory?" I barked in irritation, an irrational fear I constantly projected on him.

"No Scar, I'm questioning why you didn't listen to your gut," he snapped and turned to face me. My brother is a massive figure. His stature alone would intimidate anyone else. "You've never been wrong." Those four words kicked my ass into gear. He was right.

"FUCK!" I spit through gritted teeth. Leave it to my brother to tell me when I've fucked up.

"Everything okay?" Snake asked as he came out of the back room. My mind reeled with the possibilities of what could have already transpired in my absence. All I managed was a grunt in reply.

"We're riding out," Tank answered for me.

The roar of the engines coming to life vibrated down to my bones. The sensation was soothing and familiar.

As we rounded the bend, the service station came into view, the same silver sedan still parked on the far end of the lot. A blur—naked to the human eye—darted into the treeline at the back of the property.

We're too late!

"Snake! Follow them!"

I knew without a doubt my spy would retrieve the little bird before they could escape. That left Tank and me to follow my dove.

Wait, *mine*?

I shook my head at that thought and tried to focus on the movement through the trees as I skidded to a halt next to the sedan.

Tank transformed, his beast landed on all fours within a second. The sedan next to us was small in comparison. He tilted his head toward the open door, inhaled the scent before he took off through the trees. I followed suit and took to the skies. With my brother on the ground and me above, there was no way they could have gotten far. My brother was the best tracker we had. If he couldn't find the scent, no one could.

My gut told me they were somewhere near the ravine. The Hive has a clubhouse hidden deep within the bayou. They might have thought we didn't know about their underground bunker, they would now, but I didn't care. Instinct drove me forward, and my wings spanned out around me as I soared swiftly through the air. My brother's beast leaped the entire length of waters separating our lands. He and I must have come to the same conclusion.

Venom.

The president of The Hive MC was the reason the Legion was formed.

The entrance to the bunker came into view within minutes. My brother was already waiting in the shadows. Pulling my wings against my body, I dived toward him, shifting before my feet even hit the ground. With Snake on our side, his magic had given us the ability to shift between forms faster than the average shifter. Seconds of precious time between shifting forms could leave you vulnerable, thus this ability has put the Dark Legion one step ahead.

"She's inside," Tank said, not a sliver of doubt in his words.

I nodded and strolled straight to the main entrance, kicking the door in. The boom from the force echoed down the hall like a bomb.

Tank grinned. "Honey, we're home!" he taunted.

The hive swarmed us from all sides. My pulse quickened as the fight drew near. I lived for this shit. The rush of power and risk was the only thing that set fire in my veins.

Punching both fists into the first two that greeted me, I pulled. Then dropped the still-beating hearts to the floor. The next one caught me by surprise and latched onto my neck like a parasite. Greedy for the power my blood possessed.

Stupid blood crazed vermin.

Tank yanked the fucker free, blood pooling at the bite as the venom from their saliva coursed through my body. Deciding to return the favor, I ripped into my next opponent's neck just for the hell of it. Copper coated my tongue and fueled my beast, who roared in approval. The floor was now littered with gore and blood.

Tank's smile was feral. Blood coated his teeth, enjoying the hunt. My brother's body hummed with his beast. Unlike me, he sometimes could not control his shift. He had always seen this as a weakness, but I knew better. It was his strength. His beast had saved us countless times when no hope was in sight.

"Shift brother," I growled, hating when he held himself back.

The hall may have been narrow, but with me at his back, nothing would go unnoticed. Tank's nostrils flared briefly before he growled, so primal it echoed around us. That sound alone would send anyone running. His beast roared when he caught her scent again and took off down the hall. Around the bend we came head to head with Spider. The most vile of The Hive's worker bees.

"Where is she?" I bellowed.

Tank growled again when Spider hesitated to answer. Saliva dripped on the floor around his paws in anticipation. The need to feast on his next prey drove his beast forward. Tank took a menacing step, and Spider's face paled.

"Give her to me and we will leave," I lied.

Spider's eyes flicked to mine as he gauged if he could trust my word.

Fool.

The devilish smile on my lips must not have been convincing. In a desperate attempt to flee, Spider vamp sped around the corner.

"Big mistake," I taunted, enjoying the chase.

Tank took off around the corner and an ear-piercing scream followed. I chuckled as I leisurely rounded the bend toward my waiting prey.

"Nice try, Spider."

I crouched in front of him, his shoulder still trapped in Tank's hold. His teeth sank into the raw skin that steadily dripped with blood.

"Where is she?" my voice deadly calm as I tilted my head to

the side.

"It wasn't me, Scar. I swear! They gave me the order to bring her child here!"

He cried out again as Tank sunk his teeth in further. I wordlessly asked Tank if the child was here with a single brow raised, to which he shook his head vigorously. I chuckled at that.

They didn't have the little bird.

Watching Spider get shaken like a rag doll gave me a sick satisfaction. But I was desperate to spill his blood for myself. Raising one hand, I signaled Tank to release him. Spider fell to the floor in a sobbing heap.

"Pathetic," I said in disgust.

Gripping his bloody neck, the raw power over him gave me an adrenaline rush.

"She's in the east wing," he cried.

My grip tightened ever so slightly, crushing his windpipe. Spider gasped like a fish out of water, his eyes bulging out of his head. His face was red from the lack of oxygen. I might not be able to kill the vampire by choking him, but it sure was fun.

Tank growled in irritation that I was taking too long. I sighed and added a second hand around his neck and pulled them apart, stretching the skin until it ripped. The sound sent a shiver of arousal down my spine as a malicious smile tugged at my lips. Blood poured from his gaping mouth as he choked until I separated his head from his body.

Dropping his head to the floor, I kicked it like a soccer ball. Tank took off down the hall after it and crushed his prize between his teeth. I cackled as I watched him lick his lips in carnal satisfaction. We might be here to save an innocent, but the Dark Legion never claimed to be seeking salvation.

Chapter 3
KATRINA

A firm grip helped me sit up as my head spun. I groaned, mumbling, "I think I'm going to be sick."

Gentle hands raked my hair back as I finally succumbed to the churning in my stomach, expelling what little food I had until I was dry heaving.

"Leona," I breathed her name as a sob forced its way passed my lips.

Someone rubbed gentle circles along my back. Turning, I saw an unfamiliar man crouched down next to me. His long black hair hid his face from me.

"My daughter," I pleaded.

"Not to worry, dove. Little bird is being rescued as we speak."

I whipped my head in *his* direction and saw the MC President covered in blood.

"You?" I gasped and pushed backward on my butt until my back hit a wall, putting some much-needed space from both bikers.

"She is a pretty little thing," the one holding my hair back said from a crouch beside me.

I hadn't even heard him move, and for someone as big as him, you'd think you'd hear him coming a mile away. I scowled at him, not liking that this is the second time someone called me that today.

"Don't call me that," I snapped. I must be crazy for demanding anything from two bikers covered in blood.

"Tank," the president said in warning.

The name was fitting. Everything about this man was massive. His arms were as thick as my thighs and his eyes as dark as the night sky. I was fairly certain if he were standing he would tower over his President too.

For a moment, Tank said nothing, and I regretted my outburst. Tank wrinkled his nose as he watched me from under a thick curtain of hair.

"Why can't I call you pretty? You're a goddess." The way he said goddess made my stomach clench.

"Spider called me 'pretty little thing' too," I confess. I didn't know why I told him this, but I felt compelled to explain. The bikers exchanged a look I couldn't read. "I'm sorry but–"

The President growled and crouched before me, effectively caging me between Tank and the wall. I whimpered, closing my eyes as I waited for the strike that never came.

"Look at me, dove," the President said patiently.

He brushed my black hair from my sweaty face when I finally did. I should have been afraid of him, but I wasn't.

"I will never lay a finger on you. Anyone who does will die, just as Spider did."

My mouth popped open in surprise. They were covered in blood, but I hadn't realized they *killed* him. Footsteps echoed down the hall, pulling my attention away from the President's piercing gaze. I leaned into Tank on instinct as the President faced a new threat.

Tank pulled me closer as he continued to crouch behind me. The way he moved was graceful and feline. He wrapped his massive arm around my chest. I looked above me, his long hair tickling my face. A rose tattoo covered the underside of his chin and neck, much like the one on their MC patch.

"Don't be afraid, pretty girl," Tank breathed into my ear as his arm tugged my body closer to his.

"Snake, where is the little bird?" the President called out.

Damn, I really need to learn his name.

Another man pushed through the door with a grin on his face. This guy was smaller than the other two. Maybe five foot ten and lean, but not skinny. His head's shaved, showcasing an intricate scale tattoo along his skull and down one shoulder before disappearing under his jacket. His smile grew when his eyes found mine.

"Leona is safe with Steele," Snake answered as he walked toward me.

"Did the other parasite get away?" Tank asked, his deep voice vibrating against my back.

Snake laughed. "Naw, he never stood a chance."

"Where is my daughter?" my voice barely above a whisper.

"Come, I'll take you to her."

Snake held out a hand for me to stand, but I hesitated. His bright green eyes danced playfully as he watched me.

"Go on, pretty girl," Tank encouraged.

He slowly stood, pulling me along with him. I turned over one shoulder to look up at him. He made me feel so tiny at five foot two. Tank gave me a small smile.

"I'll be right behind you. Just have some cleaning up to do

first. Trust Snake."

Snake laughed again at that. "Naw, don't trust me, baby. My name is Snake for a reason." He gave me a playful wink, and I smiled back at him.

"Lead the way then," I said, waving him on.

Snake looped his arm through mine and led me through the trees outside what looked like a bunker. All around us was thick foliage. I'd be lost if I was alone.

"Do you know where we are going?"

"Yes, so don't worry your pretty little head 'bout it. I gotcha, and Leona is safe."

I looked over into his green eyes, expecting to see a mischievous smile, but his face was somber.

"Thank you." The words got stuck in my throat.

"No need to thank me, baby."

His serene smile returned as he unwound our arms and pulled

me into his side, making me flinch at the contact against my bruised ribs. Snake stopped abruptly and turned to face me.

"What?" I asked, glancing around the trees.

"Show me," he demanded, all traces of humor gone. His green eyes were almost glowing.

No, no way am I showing him.

"No."

"No?" He tilted his head slightly. The setting sun's rays highlighted his sharp features. I shook my head and crossed my arms.

"Your President said no one can lay a finger on me," I warned when he took a step closer, and that grin of his returned.

"I promise you when I tell him I was lookin' for injuries, he will want to see 'em for himself."

Tears welled in my eyes as shame washed over me. "Snake... Please don't."

I panicked as he took another step toward me. Just as I thought he would force my shirt up, he didn't. But instead, pulled me into his arms. His nose found the crook of my neck as he cradled me.

He assured me, "Fine, kitty Kat."

My shoulders sagged with relief. I'll deal with that later, but I was in the clear for now, and that was all that mattered. Stepping out into a parking lot full of bikes, nerves took over. Snake must have noticed, because he slowed his gait to match mine and took my hand, squeezing it slightly.

"Can I ask you something?"

"Ya just did," Snake teased.

Chuckling, I slapped his arm. He seemed to be the jokester of the club.

"Will someone be able to take us back to my car?"

"'Course someone will take ya. Why don't we get you somethin' to eat first? Hmm?"

I nodded, feeling shy.

"Come on then," he said as he tugged on my hand, leading me toward the small bar.

Every head in the bar swiveled our way. I sucked in a sharp breath at all the attention. There were at least thirty people all watching me. The men wore leather jackets, and the women were dressed in barely there clothing—some in jean shorts, some in cocktail dresses.

"Don't worry. We don't bite," Snake whispered, pushing me forward on the small of my back. When everyone returned to their conversations, it gave me a small sense of relief.

"Mama!" Leona's high-pitched voice squealed.

She darted around a waitress and rushed into me, almost knocking me over. I attempted to hide the wince, but my little girl was perceptive. I was sure the blood on my neck hadn't gone unnoticed, either.

"Hey Leona, are you okay?" I asked, pulling her into my

arms.

She studied my appearance, but didn't question me. I was relieved but also saddened that my eight-year-old was so used to seeing her mama beaten and bruised that it didn't affect her anymore.

"Yeah, Steele has been playing with me."

I followed her gaze to a man sitting at the bar. His enormous frame hunched over, and his elbows rested on his knees as he watched us.

What is it with these bikers? Every one of them is fit and large. Apart from Snake, he is short by comparison.

"Yo, Snake!" someone called out from the opposite end of the bar.

"I need to let the crew know what's goin' on. Plus, Pres will want to host church when he gets back."

Without giving me time to respond, he took off. I watched him for a moment, greeting everyone as he passed. One girl with long red hair hung off his arm as he talked to an older gentleman, who I assumed called him over.

"Mama," Leona said, tugging on my arm. "Come meet my friend Steele."

I followed behind her, feeling uncomfortable. At least she seemed excited to be here. My little girl was an excellent judge of character.

I couldn't take my eyes off Steele as we approached the bar. His smile was broad and welcoming, with small dimples that weakened my knees. His mahogany skin was flawless and smooth, with sharp cheekbones and a perfect five o'clock shadow that outlined a sharp jaw and chiseled chin.

"Steele, this is my mama," Leona said proudly.

"Hey." My voice was breathier than I would have liked.

Get it together, Katrina.

"Nice to meet you."

He held out a hand for me to take, his fingertips calloused and rough. The contrast against my smooth skin had the butterflies in my belly fluttering into overdrive.

"Leona, why don't we go get your mama something to eat?" asked an older woman with long, blonde hair.

She gave me a kind smile before leading Leona into the kitchen.

Panicking as soon as Leona left my sight, I stepped in their direction, but Steele still had a firm grip on my hand. He lifted my hand to his lips, stealing back my attention. His metallic eyes pierced mine as he laid a gentle kiss on the back of my hand. His beard tickled my sensitive skin, leaving goosebumps in their wake. My cheeks heated.

If I'm not careful, I'll get lost in those gray eyes.

"Are your eyes how you got your nickname?" I blurted.

Curling my lips inward, I bit down to avoid saying anything else. Steele threw his head back and bellowed out a laugh.

"No, sweetheart," he says, his elbow returned to his knees, bringing our faces inches apart. "They call me Steele because I'm always packing."

I looked down at the seam of his pants and then back up to a waiting grin on his face that said he caught me looking. Filled with embarrassment and on the verge of a heart attack, I took a step back.

"Would you like to see?" he teased.

His body brushed mine as he stood. I gasped at the sudden contact as he reached in between us. His knuckles brushed against my lower belly. I involuntarily took a step back.

Steele pulled out a pocket knife and laid it on the bar top. Another came from his back pocket. His boots held at least three each. Seconds later, the entire counter was littered with different size blades. My mouth hung open in shock, and he had the audacity to wink. Fucking wink.

Why is that so hot? This man is dangerous in more ways than one.

"Hey, hun, I'm Molly."

The older lady smiled as she set a plate with a burger and fries next to the knives. My eyes darted down to the plate of food as my stomach growled.

"I'm Katrina. Thank you," I murmured, sliding into the booth.

"Katrina," Steele whispered my name like he was testing how it felt on his lips.

"Steele, leave the poor girl alone and let her eat," Molly chastised. She waved at the knives and said, "And pick this up. The last thing we need is another bar fight."

My brows shot up to my hairline as I glanced back and forth between them. My curiosity piqued.

"Yes, ma'am," he said, giving her a playful salute.

He began concealing every knife again somewhere on that sexy body of his before stealing a fry from my plate. He popped it in his mouth and took off out the back exit. My mouth watered for an entirely different reason.

"I'll see you later, sweetheart."

What am I getting myself into with this MC?

Chapter 4
TANK

We walked into the bar after taking out the trash. This was the first time in months the Hive had breached our lands, but I was positive it wouldn't be the last. What I didn't understand was why they were willing to risk kidnapping in broad daylight.

How did they think they would get away with that?

"They're getting bold," Scar thought aloud, mimicking my own thoughts.

"Why her? Why now?" Their carelessness didn't make any sense.

"We should be asking *when*, not why. *When* will they try again because you and I both know they will," Scar growled.

Our fierce leader carried the world on his shoulders. Ever since we lost Rose, he had taken on more than he could handle. Even now, with this woman and her daughter. He must feel responsible for them. My brother took in all the strays, giving them a place to belong. It was in his nature.

"You're right, we need to get back and call church. There is something brewing in the air, and I don't like it." As the enforcer of our crew, it was my job to make sure the club ran smoothly and our people were protected.

Scar clapped me on the back and entered the bar first. His presence alone made every member of the club face him. Molly handed us each a beer, giving us each a kiss on the cheek. It was what she always did when we came home.

Kissing her forehead, Scar asked, "Hey grams, where are they?"

"Katrina and Leona have settled in Reap's room for the night. I thought you'd want them close."

Katrina? Beautiful name.

Scar's shoulders sagged in relief as he thanked her before heading to the basement for church. With a wave of his fingers, he signaled the main crew to follow.

Snake and Steele flanked me on either side as we sat around the table. Reap and one of our prospects entered last. They had just returned from their most recent stakeout.

"All right," Scar started, banging the gavel as he called church to order. "The Hive has attacked innocent people on our lands. We must retaliate, show them we are not to be fucked with."

Next to me, Snake chuckled. That crazy fucker had been wanting to go scope out the area for months now, but Scar and Reap had held him back.

"Snake, when Reap and the prospect are ready. You will go with them on their next run."

Snake rubbed his hands together in anticipation. "Fuck yes."

He gave me a megawatt grin, to which I rolled my eyes. Snake had good intentions, but he was impulsive and didn't think things through. Hopefully, Reap could keep him in line.

"These situations are delicate, Snake," I reminded him. He waved me off and stood.

Snake turned to Reaper and asked, "When do we leave?"

His excitement was infectious, as the rest of us followed suit. We had been planning this for months now.

"One week," Reaper grunts.

All eyes shifted to the prospect for a debriefing.

Even though Reaper was the Vice President and should be the one to tell us. He had always been the more silent type. Especially since we lost Rose.

"Well, the docks are full of empty crates. We expect the cargo to be moved that night."

Steele and I shared a look. This heist couldn't go wrong. We had too much riding on it.

"How many?" Steele asked what we had all been dreading to find out.

"At least thirty," the prospect answered. Silence befell the club as the weight of what we must do hung heavy in the air.

"Fuck," I growled as a chorus of damns and fuck mes echoed after mine.

"What about Katrina and Leona?" Steele asked next. We all looked to our Pres for an answer.

"They will stay here where we can make sure that The Hive can't access them until we figure out why they are on their radar at all. Steele, get our weapons together and make sure we're ready for next week. Tank, you're on guard duty tonight."

Scar hit the gavel against the table, signaling our meeting adjourned.

Everyone shuffled toward the door when Scar called out, "Reap. Find somewhere else to stay tonight, bro. Grams gave your room to our guests."

Reap paused mid stride, his back toward us. His shoulders tensed at this news, his gloved hand squeezed the door handle roughly. Snake and Steele both attempted to hold back laughter, but failed miserably.

We all knew how Reap felt about his space being invaded. You didn't enter his room without permission. I could only imagine how on edge this would make him, especially on a night after a stakeout. To no one's surprise, Reap said nothing as he continued his trek out of the basement.

But what Molly wanted, Molly got. You might have thought Scar ran this MC, but you'd be wrong. My grams did.

Chapter 5
KATRINA

I paced back and forth in the room Molly placed us in. Apparently, this room belonged to the club's vice president. It's pretty spacious and way too impersonal for my tastes. There weren't pictures on the wall or a shirt on the floor. Not a single item graced the top of the dresser. It was almost as if the vice president didn't live in this room at all.

I didn't know why I was so fixated on this, but you can tell a lot about a person based on their bedroom. And what did I know about this guy? Nothing. That single fact alone put me on edge. But on the other hand, I was torn. The MC had proved they wanted to help us. If there was one hard truth I knew for certain; nothing in this life was free.

It was only a matter of time before they demanded something of us in return.

The sleeping girl in the middle of the king-sized bed was my reason for living. She deserved better than the life I'd lived. Even if I couldn't give it to her, I'd be damned if I didn't fight until my dying breath. That meant we could never stay in one place too long. Never put down roots. Never truly build a life where we could be happy. My throat tightened at that realization. I'd sacrifice it all if it meant she was safe.

We had to leave tonight.

"Hey baby," I whispered. "We got to go."

Pulling her into my arms, I slunk down the hallway toward the now empty bar. My heart pounded so loudly, I was afraid someone would hear it and give us away. We had one shot at this. I refused to fail her.

I briefly glanced at the bar where Steele and I met as I inched toward the exit. God, how I wished life could have been different. Even still, I left the club and entered the unknown.

The nights here in Leesville, Louisiana, were muggy and hot at best. The air was thick with the sounds of buzzing insects. Sweat dripped down my spine, my palms were slowly losing their grip on Leona. I didn't know how much further I could carry her. It had been hours since we left and we had already stopped multiple times.

The ground was soft and spongy underfoot, making each step harder than the last. The squelching sound made it literally impossible to be quiet. Let's not forget I was completely out of breath and panting like a dog.

Buzz.

Another mosquito buzzed by my ear. Huffing, I blew my long black hair out of my face and groaned in frustration as more buzzed past my face.

"Stupid backwater bayou bullshit!" I attempted to bat them

away but with Leona in my arms it made everything more difficult. "That's it," I grumbled.

My feet were sore, my throat on fire, and I was just too fucking out of shape to be walking around this stupid lake holding a fifty-pound child.

"Leona baby, wake up."

"Where are we?" she asked sleepily.

Glancing around the trees and murky water, I tried to identify if we were even traveling in the same direction anymore. I didn't want to admit we were lost.

In the distance you could hear the haunting call of the swamp birds, their eerie cries echoed across the stagnant waters. The sky overhead was overcast, the sun just barely breaking through the thick layer of mist. I shivered at the feeling of being watched.

"We're just going to rest here for a bit. Okay? Try to get some rest. You'll have to walk for a while. You're just getting too big for me to carry," I teased while I tickled her.

Her little laughter echoed around us. My heart swelled at that sound. I opened my arms to cradle her as I watched our surroundings. After a while, my eyes slowly drifted closed. The buzzing and chirping lulled me to sleep. The faint rustling of leaves had my eyes snapping open on reflex.

My gaze darted around frantically. My heart thumped against my rib cage in a wild frenzy. There was definitely something out there. I gently shook Leona until her eyes fluttered open. I placed a finger to my lips, silently asking her to stay quiet. Standing, I put Leona between me and the tree.

Think Katrina! I need a weapon. Why didn't I take one of Steele's?

Because you were too focused on those sexy gray eyes to do much of anything else, I scolded myself.

I spotted a thick branch a few feet away and darted to grab it. Now we wait.

Fuck, I felt like a sitting duck just waiting for the slaughter. But what else were we supposed to do? Run? Where would we even go?

I had left the comforts of the MC and got us lost in the swamps. This was my fault. My breath caught in my throat as I gripped the branch tighter.

In the distance, a dark figure emerged from behind the row of trees. The breath in my lungs rushed out as three more followed right after the first. Leona whimpered in fear, hiding her face in my back.

"It's okay baby," I soothed, but it was no use. They outnumbered us. How do you explain to a child the dangers you were in? You didn't, you lied.

As the figures moved closer, they appeared to be floating along the surface. Never once slowing their strides as they got closer.

How is that possible?

My fear amplified as my brain tried to comprehend what I was seeing.

"We don't want any trouble," I yelled out. "We're just passing through."

The figure closest to us stopped just on the edge of the water that separated us, his head tilted in our direction.

"Please let us leave." I'm not opposed to begging.

I watched in horror as he took two steps back before launching himself clear across the gap and landed swiftly on the other side, like it took zero effort at all.

"What the fuck are you?" I screamed as I scrambled backwards in an attempt to avoid him.

But still the figures said nothing. Their silence was worse than if they had threatened us.Leona tugged on my hand, urging me to run. But I couldn't take my eyes off of the other figures as they too cleared the distance, one right after the other.

Taking a step back, my foot caught on the uneven terrain and

I fell backwards. I pulled Leona into my arms protectively.

"Katrina," a deep voice called out from behind me.

Looking over my shoulder, Tank was coming in fast, his long onyx hair flowed down his back in waves. A murderous look on his handsome face. This was the first time I'd ever seen him fully. He was gorgeous, but terrifying. His body coiled like a snake, ready to strike as he launched himself at us. I screamed as he leaped over us.

The nefarious growl that escaped his throat sent a shiver of fear down my spine. His body began to contort and shift. His limbs twisted and lengthened before my eyes. Fur sprouted down his hind legs to the largest paws I'd ever seen. His head and shoulders morphed, elongating into a set of snouts full of razor-sharp teeth.

Where one head once was, now there were three. They snapped and snarled in all directions. I couldn't believe my eyes. Before me stood a Cerberus. A creature of hell that I always believed to be a myth. The figures hissed and bared their fangs. Glowing red eyes glinted with hunger as they assessed the new threat. The breath in my throat caught.

Vampires.

"How is this possible?" I reached up and touched the still healing wound.

I was bitten by a vampire?

Tank launched himself at the nearest vampire, slashing out with one massive paw, tearing through flesh and bone. The vampire's scream caused the others to attack as a unit. In a blur of motion, one attacked from behind, but Tank's massive tail whipped out and sent the vampire flying through the air and crashing into a nearby tree. His body fell to the ground, but he didn't stay down for long.

The third vampire jumped up on his back, but he wasn't quick enough for the massive jaws of Tank's beast. He turned and took the vampire's head in his massive maw and chomped down, crushing it like a grape. Blood sprayed everywhere, gushing down his mouth and back.

I screamed and closed my eyes, burying my face in Leona's hair. As the chaos continued, I debated on running while both sides were distracted, but I couldn't find the courage to try.

Snarling from the battle slowly quieted down. When the sounds finally stopped, I took a hesitant look at the carnage. Tank's beast stood triumphantly over the pile of vampire corpses, panting and covered in gore.

Leona pushed up from my lap and looked around at what little was left of our attackers. My little girl should be a screaming, sobbing mess, but she is utterly calm. I know her reaction wasn't normal, but a part of me was grateful she was handling it so well.

My mouth popped open in horror as she approached Tank.

"Leona," I called out, getting to my feet. "Don't–"

Before I could finish my sentence, Leona began to scratch behind the ear of one of his three heads. His tongue lolled out of the side of his mouth as he enjoyed her attention.

This is the most bizarre thing I've ever seen.

One of the other heads licked up the side of her face, making her giggle.

What the fuck is going on?

Leona turned to the third head who whimpered at her.

"Oh no! You poor baby," she cried. "You got a boo boo."

Leona reached up on her tiptoes and laid a gentle kiss on the tip of his nose. My feet carried me closer as I stared at the scene before me in shock.

"Leona, baby," I said gently. "Why don't you come over here with me?"

Leona turned her back fully on the beast, not an ounce of fear. I pulled in a shaky breath, terrified he might hurt my baby girl.

"He won't hurt us," she said with absolute certainty.

"But how do you know?" I asked.

None of this makes any sense. How is she so calm right now?

"I can feel it mama," she said. "In here." She patted her chest, her blue eyes wide.

My brows furrowed as I tried to understand what she was telling me, but the look on her face was one of complete certainty.

"Come meet him, mama, trust me," she said when I hesitated to come closer.

Swallowing down the lump in my throat, I took another step forward. One of the beasts eyed me curiously. Familiar dark chocolate eyes stared back at me. Tank's eyes. I reached a tentative hand out in his direction and gently placed my fingertips on the side of his face. His dark chestnut fur was softer than I expected.

"This is crazy," I murmured.

Tank let out a harsh breath that washed over me, then nestled into me and closed his eyes. I let out a shaky breath of my own. A nervous laugh escaped me at how upside down my life had become.

"Thank you for saving us," I whispered, as I continued to stroke his fur. Grateful tears filled my eyes. "I don't know what I would have done without you Tank." My voice caught in my throat.

He saved us twice today and the guilt for running made hot tears fall down my cheeks. One of his beasts whimpered, and I tried to give him a watery smile.

Slowly, Tank backed away from us. Within a blink, a chiseled jaw covered in blood came into view. If someone told me the supernatural existed, I would've called them mentally insane.An unfamiliar warmth spread through me. A foreign feeling I had never experienced in all my life.

Hope.

Chapter 6

TANK

While on my patrol, I caught a whiff of Katrina's scent. Vanilla. I instantly knew she was leaving. I never gave much thought to Katrina attempting to flee in the middle of the night, but a part of me wanted to let her go. Who was I to stop a mother from protecting her child? I would not make the same mistake my father did. My beast disagreed with me, though, as I found my feet already carried me in her direction.

She was on the edge of our property by the time I caught up, heading into the thick foliage of the swamp.

What did she think she was doing going through there? She would have been better off taking the road south than pushing deeper into the bayou.

I growled in frustration, contemplating what I should do.

"I'll just follow her until she gets somewhere safe," I told myself.

Walking through the murky swamp, I wondered why Katrina would take such a dangerous route. Was it the Dark Legion MC she was running from, or something else? Despite my concern, I couldn't deny the thrill of the hunt that coursed through my veins.

Suddenly, a twig snapped, pulling me from my thoughts. I froze. Someone else was out here. I strained my senses and took in my surroundings. Other than the faint rustling of leaves and the call from the swamp birds, I heard little else outside of my racing heart. Inhaling deeply, the faint traces of old blood filled my lungs.

Vampires.

I braced myself for the fight I knew was to come. Two rushed out of the foliage, their vampire speed nothing but a blur of colors. My protective instincts took over as the first collided into me, teeth snapping in a feral frenzy. I dodged the attack, swiftly removing his heart from his chest. Two more rushed me, but I was too quick for their onslaught. Within seconds, I littered the ground with bodies.

Once the attacks had subsided, Venom appeared—the Hive's president. I watched him wearily, panting from exertion, and waited for him to make the first move.

What was he doing out here?

Never in the last eight years had I seen him on the hunt himself. He had always had minions do his dirty work.

Venom approached calmly with confidence that made me hesitant to attack first. He stopped just outside the cover of trees, keeping his distance as he studied me. His eyes scanned the carnage briefly before they flicked back in my direction.

My veins filled with hellfire, burning with hatred toward everything The Hive represented. Venom was why my life was engulfed in so much sorrow and pain. A sneer pulled at his lips, revealing his fangs.

"The woman and child belong to the Hive. If you don't leave now, I'll make sure you regret it."

I bristled at his words. "I won't let you take them."

His sneer turned into a malicious smile. "Fine, Tank. Then the girl will die, and once again, you will have no one to blame but yourself."

A scream had the birds in the trees taking flight. My heart plummeted with realization. This was all a ploy, a distraction, while his bees took my girl. I sprinted through the trees as fast as I could, begging the universe to not let me be too late. Stepping into the clearing, the vampires, one by one, jumped over the swamp that separated our lands.

"Katrina," I growled.

She was on the ground, holding Leona protectively. At my voice, she turned in my direction. The fear I saw there called to this primal side of me that was determined to protect her. I launched myself over her, landing on all fours as my Cerberus took over. Venom's threat fueled my attack. The thought of them hurting Leona had me seeing red.

I swiped out at the closest vampire, sending him sailing into a nearby tree. Another jumped on my back, infuriating my beast. My teeth clenched down on his skull, demolishing him in one bite. I growled in satisfaction as copper coated my tongue.

Katrina's screams distracted me from the next one's attack, allowing him to land a blow to my face as he attempted to blind one of my beasts. But I quickly avoided the worst of his wrath.

Once the threat was eliminated, I stood triumphantly over the bodies. I was fast enough this time. I saved them.

As Leona rushed over to me, I watched her with a mix of curiosity and caution. She was so small and vulnerable. But there was also this strength in her, which reminded me of Rose as a child. As she scratched behind my ear, a low whimper rumbled in my throat at the reminder of her loss. It's been eight years, and still, I missed her just as fiercely as the day they took her from us.

"Thank you," Leona murmured, her gaze shifted to my nose. "Oh no! You poor baby," she cried. "You got a boo boo."

Leona reached up on her tiptoes and kissed my snout affectionately. Fresh-cut roses filled my nostrils, calming my beast in a way I never expected. This new bond was filling the void of Rose's loss. My connection with this innocent soul was familial; she felt like kin to my beast. I couldn't help but feel this tenderness toward her, and I vowed to myself that I'd protect her at all costs. I wouldn't fail this time. And I'd make Rose proud.

"Leona, baby," Katrina said. "Why don't you come over here with me?"

Leona looked over at her mother. Her chin lifted in defiance.

"He won't hurt us," she said. Pride swelled in my chest at how certain she was.

"But how do you know?" Katrina asked.

I knew I should shift back and explain for myself, but my beast kept our form hostage. He insisted Katrina needed to come to terms with us in this form. Distracted by the feelings that rushed through the bond, I hadn't heard Leona's response.

"Come meet him, mama, trust me," she said.

"This is crazy," Katrina murmured.

When she gently touched my beast for the first time, a jolt of electricity ran through me. My body tensed at this new sensation. As I looked into those crystal blue eyes, my heart constricted with adoration. One that set my body on fire in a way I'd never felt before. I let out a breath of contentment. "Thank you for saving us. I don't know what I would have done without you, Tank."

Her eyes filled with tears, and I had this raw need to hold her. To soothe away the pain I saw in her broken eyes. Finally, my beast released his hold, allowing me to shift. I reluctantly broke apart from our touch and stepped back. Never once breaking eye contact. She swallowed roughly as she stared at me in awe.

Taking slow, measured steps toward her, I reached for her face, giving her a chance to deny my touch. A rush of breath released from my chest as my hand engulfed her cheek. She leaned into it and closed her eyes.

"Why did you run?" I asked her gently.

She licked her lips, her eyes settling on mine again.

"I was afraid," she whispered. My brows furrowed in confusion.

"Afraid of what?" I needed to understand.

Her mouth opened and closed as she tried to answer. Her eyes darted left and right as her vanilla scent soured with fear.

"I have to keep Leona safe, Tank." Her eyes pleaded with me to understand. "If he found us–"

My shoulders sagged in relief when I realized it wasn't me she feared. "Shh. It's okay baby, you're safe with me."

I pulled her tiny frame into my arms. A sob escaped her. Her body convulsed with each breath. My heart ached for her, and I wished I could do something to take away her pain.

I stroked her hair from her face and whispered, "Whatever you're going through, let me help you."

Her sobs came harder now, and I knew I had to convince her. I was terrified that she might run again and I wouldn't be there to protect her this time. My gaze connected with Leona's. The little girl who had seen too much. She gave me a sad smile, a look that shouldn't be on a child's face.

There was something special about these two. If the Hive wanted them, then I needed to do everything in my power to protect them. The only way I knew how to do that was at the clubhouse. The MC thrived as a unit, and I knew without a shadow of a doubt we could keep them safe. Nothing was stronger than the bond of family.

Katrina's sobs began to subside. Her shoulder sagged with

fatigue. I rubbed small circles on her back as she took a calming breath and buried her face into my chest.

"You don't always have to be so strong, Katrina. Please let me help you," I begged.

I needed her to understand how serious I was. Just when I thought she might not respond, she pulled back and looked into my eyes. I wiped the last of her tears from her eyes. Even though her face was red and splotchy, she was still breathtakingly beautiful.

She finally nodded and gave me a watery smile, a smile that changed everything.

Chapter 7
KATRINA

In the most comfortable bed I'd ever slept in, I watched the sunset on the horizon, lit the sky with soft pinks and oranges. It was nice to get a moment alone. Molly had gotten Leona a few hours ago, and I had been lying in Tank's bed ever since. After discovering the supernatural existed yesterday, I had holed up in Tank's room, avoiding everyone. A part of me felt guilty for taking over his space for so long. I felt safe here and wasn't quite ready to be social yet.

Burying my nose in the pillow, I inhaled deeply. I was quickly becoming addicted to Tank's unique scent. I couldn't get enough. It reminded me of a campfire; burning wood and smoke. There was an undertone of something sweet that I couldn't quite put my finger on. Every time I inhaled his scent, my body reacted. My hand traveled down the swell of my stomach. The ache between my thighs was almost unbearable.

Knock. Knock.

Bolting upright, I clutched the blanket to my chest.

"W-who is it?" I stuttered.

"Tank. Can I come in?"

Tank's massive frame came into view, and my breath hitched. I swallowed thickly, my throat suddenly dry. He truly was gorgeous, with bronze skin and waist-length black hair.

"Hi," I breathed.

"How did you sleep?" he asked, brushing damp hair back from his face. The fabric of his black t-shirt pulled taut against his corded muscles with the movement.

"Good. Want to come in?" I asked, feeling shy. Just being this close to him was driving me crazy.

Tank took two steps into the room and stopped. His shoulders became rigid with tension. Tilting his head slowly toward me, his nostrils flared. A sexy-as-sin smirk overtook his handsome face.

Was he smelling me?

I suddenly remembered all those shifter romances I had read. My cheeks flushed crimson, and I forced myself not to squirm.

"Dinner is in twenty minutes, and you're welcome to join us." His voice was raspy, needy, and all I could do was nod as I attempted not to express how much he was affecting me.

"I'll leave you to get ready."

Setting down a stack of clothes I hadn't noticed he had been holding, he turned toward the door. My heart drummed wildly in my chest. I didn't want him to leave.

"Hey, Tank," I said, placing a hand on his arm. Butterflies danced low in my belly at the contact. "Thank you. For everything."

His eyes softened as he looked down at me. His gaze roamed over my curvy frame. I wore a large black T-shirt, the hem falling mid-thigh. His gaze darkened as his eyes met mine again. Something primal and predatory swam in their depths.

"Anytime, pretty girl."

His words sent my heart racing. I inhaled his smoky scent. Feeling bold, I pushed up onto my tiptoes and kissed his cheek. His skin was smooth against my lips. His arms wrapped around me in a flash, pulling our chests together as my back hit the wall.

Tank's nose found the crook of my neck. His hot breath washed over my skin and sent a shiver down my spine.

"Fuck, Katrina," he growled. His lips grazed the column of my neck as he spoke. "I could smell your excitement as soon as I walked through that door...and in my shirt," he groaned, pulling me even closer. My stomach clenched at the quick motion.

"Tank," I whimpered.

My wetness dripped down my bare thighs. Tank pulled back, his eyes filled with hunger.

"Get dressed," he growled. I had to force myself to stand still under the intensity of his stare. "I'm trying to be a gentleman, Katrina, but I only have so much restraint."

Why is that so sexy?

Tank's smile was breathtaking, and if I wasn't careful, I'd fall head over heels for this man. He chuckled, knowing exactly how he was affecting me, and left me standing there feeling flustere.

While I was getting ready, I wasn't sure going to dinner was the right decision. It would be rude of me not to, especially since the club had welcomed us with open arms. Blowing out a breath to calm my nerves, I headed toward the bar. I didn't do well in large groups.

What if they don't like me?

"I can't do this," I mumbled to myself, suddenly feeling nauseous. All I wanted was to turn around and head back to the comforts of Tank's room.

The booming laughter and chatter around the corner had my steps faltering.

Great, I'm probably the last to arrive.

Nerves danced in my belly as I entered the room. Snake popped up from his seat and rushed toward me, a grin plastered on his face.

"Hey, Katrina. Hungry?" he asked, pulling me into a hug, one I hesitated to return. But that didn't stop Snake from burying his nose in my hair and groaning. The sound sent the butterflies in my stomach, fluttering like crazy. I needed to get my hormones under control. I couldn't walk into dinner with Tank being able to smell me.

"Starving," I breathed, finally hugging him back. I wasn't normally a hugger, but I couldn't deny how happy it made me.

"Good. Sit with me?"

Before I could respond, he took my hand and led me toward the table. If Snake noticed how sweaty my palms were, he didn't comment.

My eyes widened when I saw a large black crow on Steele's shoulder. Its beady little eyes watched me approach.

"That's just Cyrus, Steele's familiar." Snake said when he saw my hesitation.

"Familiar?" I questioned. "Like a witch?"

"Yes, he's a good boy too," Steele crooned, scratching under Cyrus' chin affectionately.

"Steele is a mage, kitty Kat," Snake whispered.

My mouth popped open in surprise.

I wonder what Snake is?

This entire club is nothing like I've ever seen. I felt so out of place that I wasn't sure how to respond and was too afraid to say the wrong thing.

My eyes landed on the man I hadn't met yet. His wild red hair covered most of his face, his nose buried in a book. I hadn't heard him utter a single word since I sat down. Glancing down at his leather jacket, I noticed he didn't have a patch like the others did. Just the single word 'Prospect.'

Scar sat at the head of the table, wearing a simple black button up and for once, his jacket was missing. His hands were folded on the table, giving him this air of confidence I could never muster. Everything about the MC president screamed control and calculation.

"Evening, dove. Please take a seat." My heart galloped at the nickname.

"Evening," I murmured, sitting between Snake and Steele and eyed his crow wearily.

Bursting through the double doors of the kitchen was a flushed face Leona. My shoulders sagged in relief. Selfishly, I needed my daughter as a buffer. She had always been better around people than me.

"Mama! I made dinner with Molly," she said proudly, taking a seat next to Scar.

"That's awesome, baby. What did you make?"

"Chicken pot pie."

She rubbed her stomach dramatically, making everyone around the table laugh. Her energy was infectious.

"Sounds delicious, baby.".

When Scar's piercing gaze caught mine again, I gave him a small smile. Something was bothering him, and I wished I could make it better. Show him just how much I appreciated everything he and his club were doing for us.

Molly walked in, pushing a food cart with Tank on her heels. He began laying out platters of food on the table. Once he was done, Molly pulled Tank down to her level and kissed his forehead affectionately. The sentiment was sweet, and I yearned for love like that.

Molly stopped at the head of the table and had a hushed conversation with Scar. His eyes melted around the older woman, showing just how close they were, too. I felt like I was intruding on a private moment between them. I'd only ever dreamed of the affection she showed her family. I admit I was jealous.

The club was a family; that same foreign feeling fluttered in my belly. Hope. It was a dangerous feeling to hope for something like this club had but I couldn't stomp out the feeling.

Snake nudged my shoulder with his and reached for a bread roll while Molly wasn't looking. But the woman was perceptive and slapped his hand, knocking the roll back to the table. Steele snickered from beside me, and I found myself smiling along with him. Snake gave me a playful wink, and it was then I realized he was trying to make me comfortable, and my heart soared.

"Where are your manners, son? Ever heard the saying, 'ladies first'?" she scolded him, but her words had no heat.

"I always let my lady come first," Steele whispered, his breath tickling my neck. I sucked in a sharp breath at his dirty words. A blush crept up my cheeks.

Are all of them this bold?

Steele's chuckle was criminal, and I knew I gave him the reaction he wanted. I trained my eyes on my empty plate, trying to get my racing heart under control. I was hyper-aware of Steele's every movement. My heart launched into my throat every time his leg brushed mine under the table. At this rate, I was bound to die of a heart attack.

Molly turned her bright smile on me. "Better serve yourself, quick love. These boys sure know how to eat. If you're not careful, they won't leave you any."

"Thanks, Molly. Everything looks delicious. I can't remember the last time I had a home-cooked meal."

"Hey! I helped too." Leona pouted.

"Thank you, little bird. You did a great job, I'm sure," Scar said, and Leona preened under his praise.

Tank sat down across from me, his eyes darkening when our eyes locked. A hand rubbed up my thigh under the table. My eyes darted to Steele's in surprise.

"What are you doing?" I hissed, but still I didn't push his hand away.

"Helping you relax, Katrina," Steele said.

How the hell did he expect me to relax with his hand inching higher and higher on my thigh? Tank was watching me intently, his now full plate of food ignored. His nostrils flared, and I knew he was smelling me.

Fuck. Get it together, Katrina. Think of anything else.

A small whimper escaped my lips when his fingertips ran

along the small section of skin between my shirt and jeans.

"Steele," Tank growled in warning.

"What?" he asked innocently, but he removed his hand from under the table. Steele murmured something to his crow, who flew over to a perch at the end of the table.

I gave Tank a grateful smile. I wasn't sure how to handle any of this. It seemed each one of these bikers affected me. My gaze snapped over to the prospect. Even the quiet one had something about him that drew me in. Snake scooped a few spoonfuls of chicken pot pie onto my plate and two rolls.

"Eat. Steele's just teasing you. Want me to tell him to back off?" Snake asked, all traces of humor gone. This reminded me that he knew about the bruises I had hidden and he still hadn't said anything.

"No, it's fine, thanks though," I murmured, taking a small bite.

The flaky crust melted on my tongue. The chicken cooked

to perfection and the white sauce was creamy. Delicious. I groaned in appreciation. It was better than I expected. The chatter around the table silenced, and I felt everyone's eyes on me.

"Careful making those sounds around so many hungry bikers, kitty Kat," Snake teased.

"Sorry."

Scar growled and stood up, his chair scraping against the floor, and glared at his friends.

"How many times have I told you, dove? Do not apologize." He inhaled sharply, eyes narrowed on me.

I bit my tongue to stop myself from saying it again. I didn't like seeing him so worked up. Lifting my chin, I squared my shoulders and gave Scar the most confident look I could muster.

"I'll work on it," I said. "I can't promise I'll never say it again, Scar. But I'll try, okay?"

My entire life, I'd always had to apologize, even when I knew I had nothing to be sorry for. I was weak back then, but around Scar, I wanted to be strong.

"Good girl."

I squirmed in my chair slightly, praying no one noticed how much I liked his praise.

When Snake and Steele thought I wasn't paying attention, they would lean back and talk behind my back. It was unnerving how close the two seemed. Out of the corner of my eye, I caught Snake's mischievous grin. The look directed at Steele over my head.

The exchange between the two was a silent conversation, with only their expressions. Tank glanced between the two and shook his head, taking a bite of chicken.

"Hey, prospect, you always got your nose buried in a book. Anything interesting?"

"Prospect? Why do you call him by a title and not a name?" I blurted, for some reason feeling oddly protective of this guy.

"I'm Nathaniel, but you can call me Nate."

Snake smirked and added, "He is our prospect until he earns his patch, kitty Kat. It's nothing personal. We've all been in his shoes." Turning back to Nate, he said, "What's up with the constant studyin', Nate? You plannin' on being the first Legion with a PhD?"

Nate rolled his eyes and gave me a small smile. His vibrant green eyes enthralled me. As everyone at the table relaxed, I couldn't seem to take my eyes off him.

I really needed to learn more about the club dynamics. All I knew was Scar was the president, and I had yet to meet the club's VP. My gaze shifted to the empty seat at the other end of the table.

I wonder why he isn't here?

"Nah, just trying to educate myself on a variety of subjects. Knowledge is power, right?" Nate asked with uncertainty.

Steele chuckled. "Whatever you say, bookworm. Maybe you can teach us a thing or two."

Snake leaned back in his chair and grinned. "I could use a few lessons from Katrina. We could make it a study group."

He wiggled his eyebrows at me playfully. I lowered my gaze and let my long black hair shield my face.

If these guys only knew how much they were affecting me, I'd die from embarrassment. Tank. Fuck, I bet he can smell me right now.

My eyes shot up to him across the table to find that he was already staring at me. The rigid set in his jaw combined with how tightly he held his fork told me exactly how much he noticed.

Snake turned his attention to me, one arm braced on the back of my chair with Steele mirroring his stance on the opposite side. I continued picking at my food, pretending not to notice.

"So, Katrina," Snake said, his tone feigning innocence. "How are you liking our club so far?" His green eyes sparkling with mischief.

My cheeks flushed at his question.

"Uh, it's been good. Everyone's been really nice," I answered, never taking my eyes off my plate.

Steele leaned in closer on my other side. Their combined scents are intoxicating. Snake, fresh cut grass, while Steele smelled of gunpowder. The two scents together were intoxicating. I chanced a glance in Steele's direction. There was a devilish smirk on his face, and those gray eyes pierced through mine.

"Oh, we're more than nice. I'd say we're downright hospitable," Steele said, breaking eye contact to look at Tank. "Isn't that right, Tank?"

Snake chuckled, nudging Steele in the arm behind my head. Both guys clearly enjoyed making me squirm.

"Yeah, Katrina. You've seen Tank's accommodations," Snake

whispered in my ear. "Maybe you'd like to see mine next."

My eyes widened as I sputtered, "Wh-what? I, uh, I don't know what you're talking about."

Steele tugged on a strand of my hair and whispered, "You wouldn't even have to choose, sweets. We could share you."

"Gladly," Snake added. Their hot breaths mingled with mine and boxed me in. I gasped at their nearness and their dark promises. I had never experienced anything like what they are offering.

Tank, who had been listening to their conversation from across the table, growled in annoyance. "Enough," he said, his voice low and dangerous. "Leave her alone. Nothing happened between us."

"Yet," Steele teased, high-fiving Snake above my head, who cackled like a madman.

Chapter 8

TANK

Some people started their day with coffee, needing the extra boost that caffeine offered. Not me. I always started my day off in the swamps. Seeking that adrenaline high you could only get from running. The feeling was addictive.

It gave me a chance to connect with my beast and be one with nature. I pushed myself to the brink of exhaustion. My legs felt like jelly and my lungs burned with each breath.

"Just a little further," I whispered as the club entrance came into view.

I skidded to a stop, resting my hands on my knees as I panted, trying to catch my breath. I wiped the sweat dripping down my brow with the hem of my t-shirt. Even this early in the morning, I could tell it was going to be a hot day.

"Yo Tank, we hitting the gym, man?" Nate called out. He was sitting on the front stoop with a book in his hand.

"Yep, I'm heading there now."

The guys and I liked to spar as often as possible to keep each other at our best. Taking the steps two at a time, I clapped him on the shoulder as I passed. I entered the first floor of the clubhouse, intending to avoid the morning breakfast rush and head straight to the ring. By now, the club was just rousing and would be downstairs at the bar for breakfast. Sweet vanilla washed over me.

Katrina.

My quick strides carried me in her direction. I was quickly becoming obsessed with her. Thoughts of last night's dinner filtered through my mind. Watching my club brothers tease Katrina normally wouldn't have bothered me. Steele and Snake were relatively harmless, and I knew it was all in good fun. But instinct had me almost jumping down their throats for making her uncomfortable.

"Tank," Diamond purred. Her long-blonde ponytail swayed back and forth as she ran to me. "I missed you," she breathed.

When I didn't immediately hug her back, she crossed her arms and pouted. That look wouldn't work on me anymore. My beast paced back and forth impatiently, wanting Katrina.

You and me both, buddy.

"Come on Tank, admit you missed me too," she whined.

"I told you Diamond. I'm done."

"That's what you always say, baby. But it's just a silly fight. I'm over it."

I gave her an annoyed look. I was tired of the back and forth. The last few years, we had broken up and gotten back together more times than I could count.

No more.

"I told you if we broke up again, that I was done, Diamond. Go find Snake or Steele. I'm sure they would be more than willing."

Hurt flashed in her eyes. Her nails dug into my forearm as she tried to bring her lips closer to mine.

A low growl rumbled my chest in warning. "Let go. Now."

A small whimper escaped her when she saw a flash of him in my eyes. The acrid fumes of her fear clung to her like a second skin. A part of her had always been afraid of him.

"You need to get that beast of yours under control, Tank." She spit the word with so much disgust that I couldn't hide my flinch.

She loved to use my insecurities against me. In the end, he was stronger than me. That fact terrified me. My growl was deep and feral. Those club members around us fled to avoid my wrath. Her satisfied smirk told me I gave the exact reaction she wanted. I sighed, rubbing a hand down my face.

I shouldn't have let her goad me like that.

As I took a deep breath to calm my racing heart, vanilla

invaded my nose.

My gaze darted to the left. Katrina, with a plate full of food in hand, looked completely uncomfortable. Instinct told me to comfort her, but the rigid set of her spine had me stopping in my tracks. Her eyes darted back and forth between me and Diamond. My beast whimpered at the fear in her eyes. I wished I could explain to her what she saw. But in the end, it's my fault. I let Diamond get to me.

Diamond grabbed onto my arm again. I didn't stop her, too ashamed by the hurt on Katrina's face.

"Have we met?" she asked in a tone that wasn't welcoming.

"No, sorry. I didn't mean to interrupt. I was just bringing Tank breakfast. Molly said he never comes to eat with the club and I just thought..." she trailed off, a blush crept up her cheeks.

"You didn't have to do that, pretty girl," I murmured.

Our fingers brushed when I took the plate from her. Katrina

tucked her silky black hair behind her ear bashfully. Her vanilla scent deepened with brown sugar. My mouth watered.

"After everything you did for me, it's the least I could do."

The small smile she gave me sent my heart racing. Diamond cleared her throat in irritation. Never liking when she wasn't the center of attention.

"I'm Diamond. Tank never mentioned you before," she said, rubbing herself on me like a cat claiming their territory. "You must know who I am, right?" There was a twinkle of possessiveness in her eyes.

"Oh, um, no. It's nice to meet you?" Katrina greeted.

I needed to stop this from escalating. She was like a dog with a bone. She would do just about anything when she felt threatened.

"Katrina, why don't you go find Nate? He's on the porch."

Her gaze fell at my words, understanding I was dismissing her. She gave me a nod and rushed out the door without sparing a backwards glance. My heart caught in my throat. It had to be done. Sighing, I yanked my arm and looked at Diamond in disgust. Her eyes flashed triumph, a wide grin overtaking her face.

"Diamond. We are done." I growled.

"Why, because of that slut?"

Anger flared in her eyes. I gritted my teeth to keep from lashing out again and took a deep breath to steady my nerves.

"Stay away from her."

Diamond's eyes narrowed at my threat. "Or what? Scar won't be too happy when he hears you threatening me, Tank."

Her eyes were filled with so much venom and hate. I couldn't remember a single reason why I'd ever cared for her. She was manipulative and selfish. Everything Katrina was not.

I scoffed and shook my head, not caring if she had Scar under her thumb. I was done, and she just made me hurt someone who didn't deserve it for the last time.

Chapter 9
KATRINA

A ngry tears welled in my eyes as I forced myself not to slam the door behind me.

How could I be so stupid? Tank wasn't different. Men were all the same.

"Hey, Katrina. You okay?" Nate asked. He was sitting on the ledge of the porch, one leg propping up a book while he leaned against the pillar. The early morning sun highlighted his curly red hair that was in a messy halo around his face.

"I just met Diamond," I grumbled.

Nate finally looks up from his book. His brows pinched adorably.

"Want to talk about it?" he asked, patting the railing beside him.

Sighing, I took the offered seat and looked out onto the property. It was beautiful here with the wild cypress and oak trees that lined the swamp's edge that I knew lay beyond. I shivered at what I knew lurked within the shadows.

"I don't know what I'm even doing here," I finally admitted after a beat of silence. Out of the corner of my eye, Nate flipped to the next page in whatever book he was reading.

"My entire life, I've never had a place to call home. When I was sixteen, my mom finally admitted she hated me. She drunkenly blamed me for her miserable life and couldn't wait to be rid of me."

"Ouch," Nate mumbled, but still, he never looked up from his book. Strangely, it gave me courage.

"I started saving every dollar I could from my part-time job. Well, anything I could hide from my parents." I gritted my teeth at the memories of my dad gambling away my hard-earned paychecks.

"Was it not enough?"

I shook my head.

"I had planned to run away on my eighteenth birthday and start a life of my own."

"So why didn't you?" he asked like he already knew I didn't go through with it.

I sighed and turned toward him.

"My mom guilted me into staying. She promised me everything would be alright, and I foolishly believed her."

Nate shut his book and pinned me with his emerald green eyes. I expected him to bombard me with questions, but to my relief, he stayed silent.

"When Tank said I could make a home here, I foolishly believed him, too," I said bitterly.

Nate gave me a sympathetic smile.

"You can make a life here, Katrina, you and Leona. Don't let whatever happened with Tank scare you away."

My eyes pricked with tears, desperately wanting him to be right. Feeling the need to talk about anything else, I blurted out, "What are you always reading?"

A blush slowly spread across my cheeks. I seriously needed to work on not spitting out the first thing that popped into my head.

"Well, this," he said, holding a leather-bound journal. "This is actually my journal. I started jotting down anything I found out about myself."

I furrowed my brows in confusion.

"About a year ago, Reaper found me out on a run. I had no memories of how I got there nor anything about the world we live in. All I knew was my name."

He pulled on a chain hidden beneath the collar of his shirt. A teardrop pendant with the name *Nathaniel* engraved on the side hung on the chain.

"Oh my god, Nate." I covered my mouth. My heart broke for him.

"Don't feel bad for me, Katrina. I found a family here, and I'm slowly discovering more about my powers." Nate blows out a breath. "its exciting and terrifying."

My gaze fell with shame.

Nate lost all his memories, and I'm envious. How can I be jealous of that?

Nate placed a hand on my arm, and warmth emanated through me. It felt like a warm summer day when the sun coated your skin and settled low in your bones. It was healing, and therapeutic.

Gasping, I asked, "What was that?" My voice a breathy whisper.

"I'm an empath. I felt your discomfort and just wanted you to feel better," he admitted shyly, his gaze dropping to the floor.

"Wow, that's incredible, Nate! What else can you do?" Now I was curious, on the edge of my seat.

"Well, you said Tank pissed you off, right?"

"Yeah, I met Diamond." I grimaced.

Nate wrinkled his nose at the reminder. It brought my attention to the splash of freckles on the bridge of his nose and cheeks.

"Want to see me beat the shit out of him?" he asked with a mischievous grin. "Might make you feel better?"

I eyed him skeptically.

I tried to envision quiet Nate beating someone like Tank. I snorted at the idea.

"You laugh, but you haven't seen me in action." He imitated a karate chop like a goofball. I giggled at his antics. "You have no idea what I am capable of."

"Neither do you," I teased.

Nate's eyes widened. "You wound me!" He gripped his chest dramatically.

"Nate, I was teasing. I'm so sorry." I covered my mouth to hide my shock.

Nate threw his head back and barked out a laugh. "You're probably right about that... But won't it be fun to find out?" He wiggled his eyebrows playfully. "I could be a total badass."

I slapped his shoulder in relief that he wasn't mad and laughed along with him.

"Now I'm definitely curious."

S itting on a set of bleachers, my leg bounced nervously. I had no idea what to expect from a fight between Tank and Nate. But I was definitely excited. Thank god, Molly was watching Leona. I didn't want her here. Plus, it's nice to trust someone with her and get some alone time. Ever since I became a mom, a mom was all I was.

Maybe being here at the Dark Legion clubhouse, I'll get to discover myself, kind of like Nate was.

My eyes darted over to him in the ring, bouncing back on forth on the balls of his feet while Scar murmured in his ear.

My eyes scanned the bleacher opposite of me. They were full of other members of the club. Diamond leaned against the ropes, staring up at Scar adoringly. I clenched my teeth, feeling jealous.

Is she with him, too? I heard Tank say something about Snake and Steele.

I'd never been with anyone, but my husband, and the thought of being with anyone else made my stomach turn. My thoughts turned dark as I thought of John. He was probably out there looking for us right now. I took deep, calming breaths and wiped my sweaty hands along my jeans.

I can't let him get to me. Not anymore.

"Hey, kitty Kat. Whatcha doing here, all by yourself?"

Snake leaned on the railing before me, his intricate scale tattoo on full display. Shirtless, in nothing but a pair of low-slow gym shorts. "My eyes are up here," he said darkly.

"Stop that," I snapped.

I didn't know what came over me, but I needed all the sexual tension to stop. It was so damn confusing. Steele and Snake and their sexual jokes. Nate and his easy-going demeanor. Then Scar and his confidence. Tank and his connection with Leona, plus how overprotective he was. Not to mention how addicted I was to his scent. Every one of these bikers affected me in some way.

Snake cackled at my outburst. "Hmm, so she does have some fire?"

"I'm already dealing with so much, Snake. Please, leave me alone," I said, my shoulders sagging.

The playful smile disappeared, and in its place, a sad puppy dog look that immediately made me feel guilty. He might constantly tease me, but he didn't deserve me snapping at him.

"Yeah, sure, Katrina." He jogged off toward the roped-off ring.

Fuck. Why did I have to be so mean?

I rubbed a tired hand down my face, holding back tears of frustration. I needed to apologize. Feeling determined, I jumped down from the bleachers and strolled across the room before I could talk myself out. Snake and Steele were off to the side, talking in hushed voices as I approached.

"Hey, Snake." Looking over his shoulder at me, he raised a brow but said nothing. "I'm sorry. I don't-"

The words got stuck in my throat. My eyes darted back and forth between them. My heart plummeted as I stood there like an idiot. Steele shoulder-bumped Snake and gave him a look I couldn't decipher. I stepped back, feeling dumb for walking over here without knowing what to say.

A slow smile crept across Snake's face. "The kitty Kat's got claws."

Feeling the need to defend myself, I started again. "I–"

But Steele shushed me. "Katrina. What was it, Scar said?" His eyes darted to Snake as he smirked. "Don't apologize?"

"Oh? He did say that!" Snake said with excitement. "Does that mean you need to be punished?" Snake took a step toward me.

What? Are they going to punish me? Then why were they looking at me like they would rather devour me instead?

"What?" I squeaked.

"Don't worry, sweets. You'll like it," Steele said, his voice full of dark promises. My cheeks flushed, and my stomach flip-flopped.

How do they always make everything sound so dirty?

"What do you say?" Snake asked, tilting his head as he studied me.

Just then, a bell dinged, signifying the start of the round.

"Saved by the bell, kitty Kat."

"Such a shame, sweets."

My shoulders sagged in relief. I wasn't sure I was ready for whatever it was the "terrible two" had planned for me.

Tank and Nate faced off in the center of the ring, slowly circling each other as the crowd roared in excitement. My heart pounded in my chest as Nate threw the first punch, which landed squarely on Tank's jaw. He didn't even flinch, just absorbed the blow. His tongue dipped out, and licked the small gash on his lip.

Nate followed up with a second punch. I winced, rubbing my hand across my face. The crowd erupted in cheers.

A slow smile crept across Tank's face, his bloodied teeth on full display. "You're getting faster, prospect," he praised, signaling for Nate to strike again.

I wiped my sweaty hands on my jeans again as I watched. I had seen my fair share of violence, but I couldn't seem to look away.

This time Nate didn't hesitate, his movements quick and precise. After several more exchanges, Nate stepped back to catch his breath and assessed his opponent. My pulse pounded in my ears.

"Fight back," I muttered, shifting my weight from foot to foot with nervous energy.

As the fight wore on, I couldn't help but notice Tank getting more and more worked up. His dark eyes glowed red with his Cerberus. The intensity behind his stare was powerful and wasn't even directed at me. I shivered as his nose began to elongate, and his muscles rippled with the energy of his beast.

A golden glow emanated from Nate's body. I watched in awe as giant wings burst free from his back, ripping his shirt as they expanded. The golden feathers ruffled, sending shimmering dust around the ring. Nate fluttered his wings wildly, and I felt the intense energy in the room begin to calm. It reminded me of his small touch to calm me earlier on the porch.

Tank fell to all fours, his body twisted and deformed, bones snapping as he transformed. I winced at how painful it looked. The force from Nate's wings pushed Tank's hair away from his face, coating him with the shimmering dust. Tank's body began to relax. While he was vulnerable, Nate had Tank down on the mat, his head in a viselike grip.

"Gotcha," Nate said, grinning like a madman.

Tank laughed good-naturedly. "Nice move, prospect. You were able to stop my shift this time. I'm impressed."

The tension in the air dissipated as Nate helped Tank to his feet. I let out a sigh of relief.

Nate's eyes found mine in the chaos, a wide smile on his face. I grinned back at him, proud of how he handled himself. I still had no idea what he was.

Maybe an angel?

I shook my head.

No way that is possible. Right?

Chapter 10
KATRINA

I took a sip of my coffee and glanced around the bar. The place was quiet, with only a handful of people scattered throughout the room. Most had already had breakfast. Leona was sitting beside me, happily munching on pancakes covered in strawberries and whipped cream.

"How was your day with Molly?" I asked.

Her bright blue eyes lit up with excitement.

"It was awesome! She took me out to the garden. I got to eat strawberries." She pointed at the ones still on her plate with a grin. "I helped pick these," she said proudly.

"They're delicious."

It's good to see her so happy.

Her face lit up as she glanced over my shoulder. Following her gaze, Tank and Nate strolled in. Both covered in sweat, obviously coming from the gym. My stomach dropped when I noticed Tank's right eye was black and blue. I got the urge to check if he was okay, but forced myself to stay seated. With a death grip on my mug, I watched them sit down at a table in the corner.

After how he dismissed me yesterday, I wasn't sure where he and I stood. A twinge tugged at my heart.

Why was I so disappointed he had a girlfriend? He never promised me anything. In fact, he told me he was being a gentleman.

I groaned, rubbing a tired hand down my face.

"Hello," a deep voice greeted. A guy I'd never seen before sat down in the seat beside me. "I'm Chris, you're Katrina right?"

"Um, hi," I said awkwardly.

I was not good at small talk. But this guy was cute, with long blond hair tied back in a bun. He wore a leather jacket, which I'd just found out was called a cut, thanks to Molly. He didn't have the MC wolf and roses on his.

Is he a prospect like Nate?

"I know you're new here, so I was wondering if maybe you wanted a tour? I would love to show you around. Maybe introduce you to a few of the club members."

My stomach sank at that idea. I had no interest in meeting a bunch of new people today. I had already met my quota of new faces, thank you very much.

"Oh, um." I wiped my sweaty hands on my jeans underneath the bar top.

"We could eat out in the garden for lunch," Chris offered when I didn't agree to his tour.

My gaze locked with Tank. His face was an unreadable mask, but he didn't look away like most people would when caught watching someone. No, instead he was up and out of his seat, strolling confidently in my direction. My eyes widened and flicked back to Chris.

Before I could say anything else, Tank clapped Chris on the shoulder, his eyes trained on me as he said, "Prospect, you're needed in the kitchen. Molly has dishes for you."

"What? No, I thought I was only on dinner duty?" Chris complained.

Finally, Tank broke our stare off to glare down at Chris. "Are you denying a direct order, prospect?"

Chris sighed. "No man."

He gave me a smile and took off toward the kitchen, his shoulders sagging in defeat. I felt bad for him, but also relieved I didn't have to turn him down.

"Tank!" Leona jumped off the barstool and launched herself into his arms.

"How's my favorite girl?" he said, spinning Leona in a circle before setting her back on her feet.

She giggled. "When are you going to teach me how to make a lei?"

"Soon, I promise. I have a job to do tomorrow night. After that I'm yours."

"Pinky promise?" Her face was serious as she stuck out her tiny pinky.

"Of course." Tank grinned and wrapped his giant pinky around hers. "I never break a pinky promise. Cross my heart," he said as he made an X across his chest.

My heart warmed at their interaction. Leona had never had someone like Tank in her life. Then again, neither had I.

"Now, can I have a moment alone with your mama? I owe her an apology."

Leona looked at me for a moment before looking back up at him.

"What did you do?" she demanded.

"I hurt her feelings and was a really big jerk."

Tank looked over at me when he said that, and my cheeks flushed. I wasn't used to anyone apologizing to me.

Leona was quiet for a moment as she thought. "Do you promise not to do it again?"

"I promise," Tank answered.

"Are you going to give her a pinky promise, too?" she asked in a serious voice.

"If she will give me another chance, I'll do anything she asks."

Leona nodded. "Good. Okay, I'll go see what Molly is doing."

Leona reached up and puled on Tank's shirt, as far up on his chest as she could reach, pulling him down to her level and kissed him on the cheek. I watched her skip off to the kitchen, leaving me alone with Tank. I fiddled with the hem of my shirt as I waited for him to say something.

"Wanna get out of here?" A small smile tugged at the corner of his lips.

Did I?

My stomach somersaulted.

Yes, but I found myself feeling guilty too. How could I have feelings for another woman's boyfriend?

Tank growled, interrupting my thoughts. "Whatever's going through that head of yours, pretty girl, stop it right now."

"Okay," I said. For a moment, Tank just stared at me. His nostrils flared.

"Good. Now, do you want to get out of here?" he asked again.

"Yeah, I want to go with you," I admitted as I felt my cheeks start to turn red.

Reaching out a hand, he pulled me to my feet and led me toward a side entrance. His much larger palm engulfed mine.

My heart pounded with excitement.

"Where are we going?"

"It's a surprise," he said, grinning at me over his shoulder.

Tank led me over to a row of motorcycles, and my steps faltered. Tank's brow furrowed in confusion.

"What's the matter? Having second thoughts?"

"No, it's just, I've never been on a bike before," I admitted, my cheeks flushing with embarrassment.

"Trust me, I'll drive slow," Tank said.

What if we fell? Tank would be fine, but me? I wasn't so sure.

"I have a helmet for you too, pretty girl."

He patiently waited for me to agree, and I wanted more than anything to let go of my worries. Be spontaneous for once. I nodded yes before I changed my mind. Tank's eyes lit up with excitement as he placed a helmet on my head, his fingers brushing my chin as he buckled it. The small touch amplified my already racing heart.

Climbing on, he pulled on a set of leather gloves, and the engine roared to life. He turned back to me and patted the seat behind him with an eyebrow raised, asking a silent question. With a deep breath, I climbed on behind him, wrapping my arms around his waist.

Tank reached a hand around my back, pulling me closer. I squeaked in surprise, glad he couldn't hear it over the rev of the engine. My chest collided with his back and his smoky scent invaded my nose.

He revved the engine before pulling out of the parking lot. The wind whipped through my hair as we sped down the road, leaving the clubhouse far behind.

Wpulled up in front of a run-down building and the sign up read *Legacy*. The parking lot was basically empty this early in the day. Cutting the engine, Tank tapped my thigh, signaling me to get off. My legs felt like jello from the vibrations of the bike as I stood waiting for Tank, who watched my every move as he leaned on the handlebars. I raised an eyebrow at him, but Tank just chuckled.

"You brought me to another bar?" I asked.

What was wrong with the Dark Legion's bar?

"Yeah, I thought you could use a day away from the club. Wanna have some fun? Ever played pool?"

My eyes darted to the neon sign and back to him in disbelief.

"No," I admitted. I never got to do anything like this.

"Don't worry, I'll teach you," he promised, giving me a wink.

When we entered the run down bar, an older man greeted us. "Afternoon, Tank," he said, while polishing a set of glasses from behind the bar.

"Hey, Sampson, just bringing my girl in for some pool."

My girl? What about Diamond?

My cheeks were on fire as I gave Sampson a weak smile. I really liked the thought of being his girl.

"Let me know if y'all need anything," Sampson said, before heading into the back with a tray full of clean glasses.

"Come on, pretty girl."

Tank passed me a cue and set up the game before turning his attention back on me.

"Do you want to break?" he asked.

I bit my lip nervously, shaking my head. I definitely wasn't ready to take a shot yet.

He rubbed some chalk on the tip of his cue before leaning over the table to line up his shot. His back muscles coiled as he struck the white ball. It sailed down the middle lightning fast. As the balls collided, I flinched. I wasn't expecting it to be so loud. Tank sank two on the first strike.

"Impressive," I murmured.

"Thanks. Now normally I would go again because I sank two. But this round will just be for practice." Tank came up behind me, reaching over me to adjust my hand placement on the cue. "Now, let's try an easy shot. Try hitting the seven in the corner pocket," Tank said and pointed.

"Easy shot?" I scoffed. There was no such thing as an easy shot for me.

"Don't worry, I'll show you," he chuckled, his breath tickling my neck.

I swallowed roughly at his nearness, trying to concentrate on what he was showing me. Tank gently guided my fingers until I lined up the shot.

"Okay, now take the shot," he whispered, stepping back to give me space.

I took a deep breath to calm my nerves. I really wanted to

impress him. I missed, and Tank chuckled.

I frowned. "Don't laugh. I was distracted!"

More like "dick-stracted".

"Relax," he laughed again, placing a hand on my shoulder and spinning my back toward the table. "It's just a game, pretty girl. Let me show you again. Like this," he said, taking another shot.

"Okay," I huffed. "I got this." I bounced on the balls of my feet as I prepared to try again. Tank shook his head, laughing at my antics.

I took the cue and leaned over the table. This time, I went for my own shot. Tank stepped behind me again, his chest pressing lightly against my back as he guided my hands once more.

"Relax your grip a little," he murmured.

Tanking a deep breath, I aimed. The cue hit the white ball and sailed it into the two-ball. I didn't make the shot, but I didn't care. I was having fun.

"Yes!" I cheered, throwing a fist in the air in triumph.

"You're a natural," Tank teased, a giant grin on his face.

He looked so handsome at that moment. A blush crept up my cheeks as he leaned an elbow on the table, bringing our faces inches apart.

"Thanks for being patient with me," I said, tilting my chin up toward him.

"Of course," he replied, brushing my hair hack from my face and for a moment I thought he was going to kiss me. "Okay, let me show you how it's done."

We reluctantly broke apart, and I rounded the table to the other side. Leaning back against the wall, I watched him call his shots. I wasn't paying attention to how he was actually lining up his shots.

I wonder how his lips would taste?

"Okay. Are you ready to try again?" he asked, interrupting my thoughts.

I blushed and nodded. Taking a deep breath, I lined up my shot. This time, I hit the ball, and it sank smoothly into the corner pocket. It was a relatively easy shot, but still. A win is a win.

"Yes!" I cheered, turning to face Tank with a satisfied grin. "I did it!"

"Great job, pretty girl," he said, grinning back at me.

I felt a warm feeling of pride spread through me at his praise.

"You hungry? I bet Sampson wouldn't mind if we found something to eat."

"Sure, all I've had is coffee." Tank gave me a disapproving look, but didn't comment.

Taking my hand, he led me in through the double doors of the kitchen.

My eyes widened. "Tank, we can't just go back there." Tank chuckled again. "Stop laughing at me," I exclaimed.

Tank held up a hand. "The club owns this bar, pretty girl. It's fine, I promise."

I let out a sigh of relief. "Why didn't you just say that?"

"You didn't ask. I'm not trying to overwhelm you, okay? But just know you can ask me anything," he said.

Following him into the spacious kitchen, I found a seat at the small table. Tank headed to the pantry, grabbed a loaf of bread, and tossed it on the counter. Next, he gathered ingredients from the fridge for sandwiches.

"So what happened to your eye?" I asked. I had been wondering since this morning when he came into the bar with Nate.

Tank grinned. "Nate happened," he said simply.

I shook my head. I hated seeing him hurt. "Why do you not fight back when spared yesterday?"

"How can I expect the prospect to get any better if I don't build his confidence?"

I thought about that for a minute, and I wished I knew how to defend myself.

"Maybe you could teach me sometime?" I asked.

Tank's eyebrow rose at my question, and I was sure he was going to deny me.

"I think that's a great idea, pretty girl. We could start tomorrow."

I smiled softly, grateful he was willing to teach me. Maybe with his help, I could defend myself when the time came. My mind drifted to Diamond again. Before this went any further, I needed to know.

"Hey Tank, can I ask you something?" I drummed my fingers on the table. "Is Diamond your girlfriend?"

Setting down an arrangement of cold cuts and cheese, he faced me. "She's my ex. It's over between us. I've known for a while now that I didn't want to be with her anymore."

"Does she know that?" I asked, remembering how territorial she was with him.

"She does. I promise you, we haven't been together in months."

I nodded, not really sure what to say to that. I didn't like the idea of him being with anyone else. Tank growled, closing the distance between us. He tilted my chin up and forced me to look into his eyes.

"Tell me what's going through that head of yours," he demanded.

"N-nothing," I stuttered, afraid I'd sound crazy if I told him how I felt.

Tank's eyes narrowed into slits, his nostrils flaring. I averted my gaze to anything but him. His thumb drew small circles along my jaw when I hesitated to answer.

"Katrina, look at me," Tank said softly. "Please."

Looking into his dark brown eyes melted my resolve, and I blurted it all out. "I'm jealous, okay? Is that what you want to hear? Seeing her hang all over you drove me crazy."

I tucked my lips between my teeth to stop myself from saying anything else. Tank spun my chair to face him fully, bracing his hands on the table, and caged me in.

"Want to know why it's over for good this time?" he asked. I licked my lips and nodded, words evading me. "I met you."

"What?"

I put a hand on his chest, silently asking for space. Tank's shoulders sagged, but he took a step back. I stood and started pacing back and forth.

Am I the reason they broke up?

In a flash, I'm backed against the wall, Tank towering over me. His nose was in the crook of my neck. This time, I didn't have the strength to push him away. His hands found my hips, giving them a gentle squeeze. My stomach clenched in anticipation.

"Did you forget that I can smell you?" he murmured, his lips brushing against skin. I sucked in a sharp breath. "Every time you feel nervous or upset, I can smell it on you."

"I can't be the reason you broke up, Tank. I just can't."

Tank leaned back slightly. "I don't want her. I want you."

His lips crashed against mine. I gasped at the sudden contact. Tank licked the seam of my lips, and I felt my body get hot. He groaned when I opened up for him. His fingers gripped my hair harder, demanding more. His hard body pushed up against me as he continued to devour me in a passionate kiss.

Finally, he pulled back, both of us panting. A slow and sensual smirk crossed his face. "Damn, I've wanted to do that ever since I saw you in my t-shirt."

His eyes darkened with lust. I blushed at the memory.

"Me too," I admitted.

"Sandwich?" Tank asked, raising a brow playfully.

I laughed, nodding. Maybe there *was* something between us.

Chapter 11
TANK

"What do you mean, the shipment hasn't arrived?" Scar's voice boomed.

"I sent Cyrus to scope out the area last night and the entire operation was gone. No crates, no lackeys, nothing. It was like they just packed up and left," Steele said, as he ran a hand through Cyrus' feathers.

"The entire operation was counting on them being there tonight. Why would they just leave?" Scar runs a hand through his hair in frustration. "It doesn't make any sense," he mumbled, flopping down into a chair at the head of the table.

"Pres, we should just go to the drop site. What's the harm in at least showing up?" Snake suggested.

I exchanged a look with Reaper, him and Nate had been tracking them for weeks now. If anyone had an idea what happened, it was them. I raised an eyebrow in question, but Reaper's eyes just narrowed in response.

"If the Hive is expecting us, then we could be walking into a trap," Scar said.

"So send Cyrus and Snake in. One on the ground, one practically invisible," Steele offered.

It's a move we had done a thousand times in the past to gain intel. But something told me if they already knew we were coming, then they would expect a crow in the sky.

I shook my head. "I don't think that's a good idea, Steele. What if they've got some kind of new magic that can detect Cyrus or Snake?"

Scar sighed heavily. "He's got a point. We can't afford to take any unnecessary risks."

"But what other choice do we have?" Snake interjected, always willing to spy. "We need to know what's going on with that shipment. If we don't, we could be looking at a major setback for the entire operation."

Prospect leaned forward, his voice low and urgent. "I say we send in one man to do some recon. Someone they wouldn't expect. See what we can find out."

Scar nodded slowly. "Okay, but who do we send? We can't just send anyone. This is a delicate situation, and we need someone that can track the shipment."

All eyes turned to me, and I felt a sudden surge of anxiety. Everything we had worked for relied on this moment. Plus, going in blind was a risk.

"I'll go," I said, my body coiling with anticipation. I could feel my beast pacing back and forth, ready for a fight if it came down to it.

Scar looked at me for a long moment, his expression unreadable. We couldn't afford to lose anyone else. He nodded once.

"Okay, you're up. But be careful and stay in touch. We'll stay in the shadows nearby, just in case you need backup."

Meaning, if shit hit the fan.

My heart skipped. Everyone was relying on me. If I couldn't pick up the scent and figure out what was going on...

Scar banged the gavel and, as I rose from the table, I felt a mixture of nerves and excitement. This was what I'd been training for, what I'd been working towards for eight years. It was time to put my skills to the test. Prove that I was worthy of my place at the table.

As I exited the basement, I saw Katrina was standing awkwardly off to the side, an unsure smile tugged on her lips. She wore a black pair of sweatpants and an oversized t-shirt.

"Morning, pretty girl. Were you waiting for me?" I asked, pulling her flush against me. Her sweet scent washed over me, calming my nerves.

"I thought you said we were doing a training session today?"

she asked shyly.

I had completely forgotten my promise to teach her self defense. But now that I was going into the stakeout tonight alone, I had to teach her today. If anything went wrong, I needed Katrina to be able to defend herself.

"Of course we are. Are you ready now?"

She nodded, letting our hug end all too soon. Feeling the need to keep her close, I draped an arm over her shoulder as we walked toward the gym at the back of the property.

"Everything okay?" she asked.

Glancing down into her crystal blue eyes, I tried to force a smile, but I must have missed the mark. A frown tugged at her lips as she studied me.

Feeling the need to reassure her, I said, "It's a club business. I'll be leaving tonight, and hopefully I'll be back by morning."

I couldn't share any club business outside the immediate circle. Especially since there was a mole in the mix. We couldn't have this information leaking outside the club.

"You're leaving?" Her voice was small and vulnerable and I didn't like being the reason she would worry.

"Don't worry, pretty girl. I'll still be back to do your training session in the morning." I said, kissing her on the forehead.

The gym was bustling with people, and Katrina's back stiffened. Her scent told me how uncomfortable she felt around the large group.

Leaning into her ear, I murmured, "Want me to kick everybody out? I totally can, you know."

Katrina gasped, her eyes widening in horror.

"Because of me? No, no, please don't do that." She shook her head fiercely.

"Okay, okay," I said, miming zipping my lips shut and throwing away the key.

Katrina smiled in amusement, bumping me with her shoulder

as we continued our trek over to the sparring mat.

I wouldn't really have kicked everyone out. But it did work to get Katrina out of her head. Already her shoulder was back and head held high as she marched over to the mat with determination in her strides. I chuckled. I loved seeing her slowly come out of her shell.

"Tank."

My back stiffened. I watched Diamond jog over, a bright smile on her face. My eyes narrowed with suspicion.

"What do you want?" I grumbled.

"Oh, um, I just wanted to apologize to Katrina." Her gaze shifted between us. "I'm really sorry for how rude I was to you a couple of days ago. But I talked with Scar and I swear, I'm completely over the whole thing."

I rolled my eyes. All she had ever cared about was if *she* was over it or not.

"It's okay," Katrina said, giving her a kind smile. She really was too nice.

"So, are you here to spar?" Diamond asked. "I could totally use a partner."

Katrina's eyebrows shot to her hairline in surprise, and a blush slowly spread across her cheeks. She looked totally beautiful when flustered, and my cock jumped as an image of her flushed for an entirely different reason flashed through my head.

"What do you say, Tank?" Katrina asked me. I wasn't listening to either of them, so I had no idea what she was asking me.

"Yeah, sure. Whatever you want, pretty girl," I agreed easily.

Diamond squealed in excitement. "Oh, this is just perfect!" she said. "I never get to spar with someone who isn't one of the guys."

Katrina grinned at that, and my brows furrowed in confusion.

She wanted to spar with her? This wouldn't go well.

Chapter 12

KATRINA

D iamond seemed nice enough, and to be honest, I was excited to have a girlfriend. I'd never really had time for one growing up. At 35, that was kind of sad, but better late than never, right?

"Come on," Diamond said in excitement, grabbing my hand and pulling me onto the mat. It was a lot bouncier than I thought it would be. Which was good, because knowing me, I'd probably end up on the ground more times than I'd like.

Tank held a roll of tape in one hand. "Safety first."

He beckoned me closer and my upper lip began to sweat.

Was I really doing this?

Tank leaned in close to me while he wrapped my hands in

blue tape, his breath warm on my ear. "You don't have to do this, you know?" he whispered. "We could train somewhere else."

My eyes darted to Diamond, and she gave me a friendly grin. I wanted to do this, no; I needed to. This was to prove something to myself Prove that I was strong enough to handle this. Feeling a flutter in my chest, I straightened my spine.

"I want to do this," I said firmly. "Tank, I have to learn how to fight. I'm tired of feeling helpless."

His eyes softened. "Okay, pretty girl. But if it's too much for you, we'll stop."

I sighed in relief, giving him a small smile. I needed him to teach me, but I wasn't quite ready to fight him.

Diamond walked over, a confident smile on her face. "Ready?" she asked, and I felt a surge of excitement.

"As I'll ever be," I said, gnawing on my lip.

"I'll go easy on you." A mischievous smile played on her lips.

"Until you get the hang of it."

"Alright, first things first," Tank said, "Your form."

He demonstrated the basic boxing stance, lifting his hands into a loose fist, his right foot forward, knees bent. I tried to mimic him, but felt clumsy and awkward. My eyes darted to Diamond. She seemed to know what she was doing, and I suddenly questioned if I could do this.

"Katrina," Tank said, getting my attention back to him. "You got this."

Inhaling sharply, I lifted my hands again. "Like this?"

"Good, that's it. Keep your arms up," Tank said, pushing my fist up slightly near my face. "Ready to start with some basic moves?"

I nodded, licking my lips nervously.

He turned to Diamond. "Why don't you show us a jab?"

Diamond stepped forward and threw a quick punch. I

watched closely, trying to memorize the movements. I wanted to do well today.

No pressure.

My heart pounded in my chest when it was my turn. Taking a deep breath, I threw my first punch and a bubble of laughter bursted from my chest. It felt weak and awkward. I started to second guess myself.

"Try to keep your arm tighter and snap your punch a bit more," Tank suggested, seeing my struggle. I smiled at him gratefully and tried again.

By the time Tank had gone over a few different punching techniques, I was already out of breath. Sweat poured down my forehead. Nerves hit me again as I watched Diamond's execution. It was obvious she was a skilled fighter.

"Alright. Are you ready to give it a go?" Tank asked me.

"I'll go easy on you, Kat," Diamond reminded me. I nodded, stepping up and resuming the stance Tank had taught me.

"I'm going to have Diamond throw the first punch. All I want you to do is try to block it."

"Ready?" Diamond asked.

I nodded and braced myself. I flinched as my side took the brunt of Diamond's first punch. But to my surprise, it didn't hurt as bad as I thought it would. She really was holding back for me.

"Again," I called out, more confident.

The next few punches came faster, and I was able to block one with my forearm.

Fuck, that one hurt.

I shook out my arm as I bounced on my feet. The rush of adrenaline was addicting.

"You're ready," Tank stated matter-of-factly.

I grinned and threw my first punch, to which Diamond easily blocked it.

"Oh, come on Kat. You can do better than that," she taunted.

Determined to prove myself, I gritted my teeth. I launched into my next punch, catching Diamond in the jaw. I gasped and covered my mouth as regret immediately set in.

"Oh my God, Diamond, I'm–" A punch landed on the side of my face.

"Don't fucking apologize." Diamond laughed, bouncing on the balls of her feet. "I won't," she said, taking another swing, one I blocked easier this time.

She signaled me to go again, and I pushed into the next few punches as best as I could. As the minutes ticked by, I felt more comfortable, more confident in my movements.

"Alright, let's break," Tank called out.

Both of us lowered our hands, panting to catch our breaths.

"That was great," I said, grinning from ear to ear.

"You did good, newbie," Diamond teased, bumping her

shoulder with mine.

"Thanks."

I knew with Diamond and Tank, I was bound to get better.

Chapter 13

TANK

The crisp evening air whipped my hair against my cheek as I sped down the back roads. Gripping the handlebars tighter, I revved the engine—the crew flanked behind me. Everything was riding on tonight. But ultimately, it was up to me to see this through. We needed this win. Rose's beautiful smile filtered through my mind and that familiar ache settled in my chest. The Hive needed to pay for what they did to her.

As we rode toward the docks, I couldn't help the nervous energy coursing through me. My Cerberus paced back and forth, ready to spring out at a moment's notice. Something about this entire mission didn't sit right, but I refused to give up. People's lives were at stake, and it was up to the Dark Legion to serve justice once and for all. We couldn't let anyone else suffer because of the vampires.

I was always willing to die for our cause if it meant Rose saw justice, but now I found myself hesitating to be so reckless in my revenge. I made a pinky promise to Leona. One that I refuse to break. She had already had the world fail her and I couldn't—no, I wouldn't be another who disappointed that little girl.

Then there was Katrina. I didn't know what she was running from, but I wanted to keep her safe more than anything. My heart seized as my imagination ran rampant. The horrors my pretty girl must have endured to put such fear in her eyes. The same look I saw in Rose's eyes the day she died. Determination pushed me further. If I could do this, then maybe I could be worthy of her. She deserved that much.

I signaled to the others that we were arriving and slowed my bike to a stop. Scar pulled up on my right, and Snake was on my left. I shared a look with both, and I could see the fear and determination in their eyes, one that mirrored my own. I nodded to Snake, who slowly got off his bike to follow me.

"I need you to do me a favor," I said in a low voice.

Snake's brow furrowed, his arms crossed over his chest. "Name it."

"If this goes south, I need you to take care of Katrina. I promised to teach Leona how to make a lei and I need you–"

Snake held up a hand to stop my rambling. "No, you're comin' home today, Tank. I don't wanna hear you talkin' like that."

I growled, pushing my hair from my face in frustration. "Just promise me, Snake, please." For a moment, he didn't respond, and I feared he wouldn't say anything else.

But then he whispered, "Always, brother. You're not the only one who cares for them, ya know." My shoulders sagged in relief. Snaked pulled me into a hug. "So, you kinda fallin' for our kitty Kat?" he teased.

I chuckled. Snake was always the jokester.

"I'm serious though, Tank. We are all goin' home today, and

you can teach lil Leona how to make a lei yourself."

Nate stood off to the side, a worried look crossed his face as he surveyed the swamp surrounding the warehouse. Our eyes locked. "Don't worry, Tank. We can do this," he said.

His golden wings fluttered slightly. A calming breeze washed over us. Instantly, my body relaxed. Glancing around at the others, I saw that Nate's abilities were having the same effect on them, too.

"Thanks, man," I said.

"Anytime," he said with a small smile. "We're in this together."

Scar clapped Nate on the shoulder. "You did well." To me, he said, "You're scoping out the area while we hang back. Signal us when you're ready and we'll be right behind you."

Brushing my hair from my face, I looked down to his president's patch, and I patted my own—a wolf surrounded by a cluster of roses. Reminding me of how much stronger we were when together.

"I know you said I should go in myself, but I think we should go in together. All of us."

Snake and Scar exchanged a look.

"Steele, send Cyrus in ahead," Scar directed.

Steele whispered something into his familiar's ear as we made our way to the warehouse. Cyrus took flight, soaring overhead to scope out the area for any signs of the Hive's operation or the shipment. His eyes glowed with a deep shade of purple as he scanned the surroundings. Suddenly, he let out a sharp *caw*. Feeling uneasy, I scanned the treeline. My skin prickled with awareness.

"There's movement inside," Steele reported, his voice low and tense. His eyes turned magenta as he used his familiar's sight. "I can see at least two guards posted inside."

My heart raced as we crept closer to the back entrance. The dim light overhead cast eerie shadows on the boxes stacked high around us. Being out in the open like this was putting everyone on edge, and even Nate's calming gift didn't seem to help. The air was thick with the musty scent of rotten food, making it difficult to catch my breath.

"Wait," Snake said, halting us from walking forward. "I can sense magic. It's faint, but it's there."

With a wave of his hand, Snake used his jinn powers to conceal our presence, making us practically invisible to any potential threats. I was grateful for his abilities, which had saved our hides more times than I could remember.

Despite Snake's powers, my palms were slick with sweat, and I couldn't shake the feeling of being watched. Every creak and rustle the old building made had me jumping.

I was completely on edge by the time we made it into the building. Steele and Nate walked in first, Cyrus flying in ahead to survey the building. My eyes darted to my brother. Scar took up the rear, always watching our backs. All of us were tense in our movements, but Snake remained calm and focused, his jinn powers holding strong and keeping us hidden from prying eyes.

Reaper suddenly appeared beside us, his scythe at the ready, his hands glove free. My breath caught at the sight. I knew how much he despised this side of himself.

"Be on your guard," he said in a low voice. "Something isn't right."

As we arrived at another door, I held up a hand, signaling for everyone to halt. My senses were on high alert as I listened for any sounds beyond the next door. It was eerily quiet, which only added to my unease. I shot a quick glance at Scar and he gave me a nod, silently agreeing with my unspoken plan.

With a deep breath, I pushed the door open, and we stepped inside. Cyrus swooped and landed on a windowsill, surveying the area. My nerves settled slightly. Nate fluttered his wings again, calming everyone as we rounded the corner and came face to face with a large metal door guarded by two heavily armed men. They turned to face us as we approached, their weapons raised and ready to fire.

"Stay back," one of them growled. "This area is off limits."

"It's your unlucky day, boys," I taunted. "Move or die."

The guards sneered, but before they could react, Snake stepped forward, and his eyes glowed a deep blue. The intricate snake-like tattoos that covered his arms and shoulders shimmered and slithered. It made them appear alive as he tapped into his magic. He whispered something under his breath, and suddenly the guards' eyes dulled before they slumped to the ground, asleep.

"You never let me have any fun," Steele huffed, flipping a blade with expert ease.

Rolling my eyes, I pushed open the thick metal doors, surprised to find them unlocked. It seemed all too easy, almost as if they knew we were coming.

Cyrus flew overhead, his sharp eyes scanning the area for any sign of trouble. The warehouse was dark and quiet, with rows of crates stacked high on either side. Inhaling deeply, I couldn't pick up on any specific scents. Almost as if we were alone here, but that wasn't possible, as we just left two guards at the door. At the very least, I should have been able to smell them. Yet another red flag.

"Be on guard," I whispered to the others. "Something doesn't feel right."

We crept forward, our footsteps the only sound against the concrete floor. The rows and rows of crates were eerily silent.

Were they empty?

A figure stepped out from behind a stack of crates, his ruby eyes glowing in the darkness.

"Get down!" I shouted, as I launched myself forward, shifting before my feet hit the ground.

The vampire fired his weapon, but Steele was too quick, and knocked it aside with a quick toss of a throwing knife. The vampire screamed out as the blade embedded into the palm of his hand, and his gun clattered to the ground. Steele's crow swooped down, his talons raking across the vampire's face, blinding him. Nate fluttered forward, his wings beating furiously. The vampire's eyes went wide as he stumbled backwards, his expression morphing into confusion.

Reaper appeared in a cloud of thick black smoke, his scythe gleamed in the dim light. He swung it down, and the guard fell to the ground, his body disappearing in a cloud of black smoke. My Cerberus growled in frustration, wanting to be the one to deliver the final blow.

Murmuring caught my attention, and I took off to investigate. I rounded the corner and Venom stood before me. A low, menacing growl tumbled from my throat.

"Tank, so nice of you to join us," he said with a sneer.

Beside him stood a petite girl, her long black hair shielding her face from view. Inhaling deeply, a familiar scent hit my nose.

Rose.

Without hesitation, I charged towards the girl, my heart pounded in my chest. A nagging voice in the back of my mind told me that something was wrong. But my Cerberus had control. All he wanted was to reach Rose.

We pushed the thought away, our mind consumed by the smell of eucalyptus and rain, and the need to protect *her* at all costs.

Venom suddenly lunged forward, unsheathing a sword. He lifted it above his head and swung downward. I barely managed to dodge in time, and I switched my focus to defending myself. His sword connected with the concrete floor. The force of his blow shattered it like glass.

Chaos erupted. The Hive swarmed in from all sides. In the distraction, I lost sight of the girl and Venom.

Damn it.

They outnumbered Nate and Steele. A swarm of five or more vampires cornered them. Scar and Reaper were fighting their way through the masses, slowly making their way over.

Where is Snake?

An ear-piercing scream pulled my attention from the battle. Snake crashed into a row of crates, knocking them on the ground as he fell. Launching myself across the warehouse, I shifted back to my human form, ignoring the surrounding chaos. I had to focus on getting my crew out of here alive.

"Snake, we gotta get you out of here," I said, feeling a lump form in my throat.

Blood seeped from a gash on his leg, and his movements were slow and labored as he tried to sit up. Guilt burned in my chest. I had failed to protect him.

"Looks like you get to make a lei after all," Snake said.

"Shut up," I said with a smirk.

He winced as he slowly got to his feet, favoring his right leg. Quickly, I looped my arm under his and helped him to his feet, trying my best to be gentle as he let out a low groan of pain.

"Fall out!" I bellowed over my shoulder.

Making our way towards the exit. Steele and Nate were right on our heels. Snake leaned heavily on me as we limped along the hallway. Every step seemed to be agony for him, and I felt another surge of guilt wash over me.

As we burst out of the warehouse and into the night air, I couldn't help but feel like we had failed. We had come so close to finding the girls, only to be ambushed by the Hive. I lowered Snake gently to the ground and examined his wound. I released a breath. Thankfully, it wasn't life-threatening.

"It's not that deep," I reassured him, ripping a strip of fabric from my shirt.

"That's what she said,' Snake joked.

I rolled my eyes, making him laugh. With my shirt, I applied pressure to stop the bleeding. Snake winced, but didn't protest. I gritted my teeth in frustration.

How could I be so stupid but to think that girl was Rose?

Rose died six years ago, and she was never coming back. And now, one of our own was injured because of my mistake.

"It's not your fault, Tank," Steele said, coming up behind us. I gave him what I hoped was a reassuring smile as I helped Snake back to his feet.

"You okay to ride Snake? Or do I finally get to make you my bitch?" Steele grinned at his best friend.

"Ouch," Snake chuckled. "I'm not gonna leave my bike. I'll be fine."

Steele's face went serious as he assessed Snake's leg.

"You tell me if you can't. I'll make sure your bike gets back."

Snake nodded, looping his arm around Steele's neck, and limped off toward our bikes. Scar and Reaper burst through the back door, a swarm on their heels.

Shit.

I took off toward my bike, revving the engine, as I waited for the rest of the crew to do the same. We sped off down the road, leaving the vampires in a cloud of dust and rubble.

We would regroup and try again. And this time, we would be ready for whatever the Hive had in store for us.

Chapter 14

TANK

All I wanted was to fall into bed and pass the fuck out. Forget today's epic failure. Swinging the door open, a wave of flowers and spice washed over me. I swallowed thickly, my mouth suddenly dry. My gaze snapped to Katrina's sleeping form sprawled out on my bed. Licking my lips nervously, I debated on waking her.

My gaze trailed down her curves, a leg exposed from beneath the tangled bed sheet—long black hair in a messy halo. The covers twisted around her torso. My breath caught.

She really was beautiful.

My heart pounded in my chest as I memorized her curves. I felt like a total creeper watching her sleep, but I couldn't find a reason to care.

I looked down at my hands covered in Snake's blood. I didn't want her to be upset if she saw me like this—or worse—see fear in her eyes. With a sigh, I draped my cut on a chair before shedding my tattered t-shirt and slipped off my boots. Never once taking my eyes off my pretty girl.

My Cerberus shifted within me, agreeing with Katrina being ours. I smirked. She was mine the moment I caught her scent on the breeze the day the Hive took her. My smile faltered at that thought, knowing we failed to stop them. Again.

The floorboard creaked as I stepped toward the bathroom. I paused, glancing over my shoulder at my sleeping beauty. Thankfully, she didn't so much as stir. I let out a breath of relief and stepped into the bathroom. The door closed with a soft click.

Stripping out of my jeans, I stepped into the blazing shower. The spray soothed my aching muscles. I closed my eyes with one hand resting on the cool tile wall. Katrina's bright blue eyes came into focus. Seeing her in my bed was a welcomed surprise.

Was she naked underneath all those covers? Wearing one of my shirts?

I growled at the thought. Imagining her curves on display through the thin white fabric, her nipples pebbling under my stare. I groaned, gripping my aching cock in my fist.

"Tank?" a soft voice asked.

My eyes sprung open. Katrina stood in the doorframe, her eyes widened, her luscious lips parted in a silent O. Slowly, I stroked myself, her breasts rising and falling with each sharp inhale as she watched me. A small pink tongue darted out and licked her lower lip.

The navy blue top dipped low on her ample cleavage and the shorts revealed thick thighs. My mouth watered at the sight. I had the sudden urge to sink my teeth into her creamy skin, mark her, claim her. I stroked myself faster.

Her pale cheeks flushed crimson when our eyes locked. I smirked in satisfaction, rubbing a thumb across the head of my cock.

"See something you like, pretty girl?" I asked huskily.

Her eyes darted around the room. "Y-you're back," she stuttered.

Snapping out of her lustful haze, she bumped into the doorframe in her haste to run away. My stomach clenched in anticipation.

"You trying to run away again, Katrina?"

"What?" she squeaked.

I shut off the tap and stepped out of the stall. I stalked toward her, and water dripped on the tile floor.

"If that's the case, I'll chase you. Again." I chuckled darkly.

"Tank, I–" she started, her mouth opening and closing as the words caught in her throat. She took a step back, then another, until the back of her knees hit the mattress, forcing her to sit on the edge. Slowly, she looked up at me from under her lashes. Her throat bobbed as she swallowed.

"Why are you in my room? Did you miss me?" I teased, a smirk playing on the corner of my lips.

"I'll just go?" she said like a question, her eyes darted to my still-hard cock.

She shifted her thighs together as she stared. Caramelized brown sugar wafted from her. I groaned, pushing my wet hair back from my face.

"Fuck Katrina," I growled, "I've been trying to be a gentleman, not push you too far too fast. But coming home and finding a goddess in my bed? A man can only resist so much."

She scoffed, crossed her arms over her chest, and turned her head to shield her face with a curtain of raven locks. I growled again, not liking that she was hiding from me. So I knelt before her, but still, she refused to look me in the eye. I gripped her jaw gently, stroking her cheek. My heart caught in my throat when my thumb came back wet with her tears.

"Why are you crying, pretty girl?" I asked softly.

"Stop that!" she demanded, turning her furious gaze back to mine. "Stop telling me I'm pretty, Tank. Diamond and I look nothing alike. I've never been a pretty girl. I'm short and have always struggled with my weight."

She laughed bitterly. "I was okay with that until I met you. Stop telling me I'm pretty because I'm not. Stop saying I'm a goddess, I'm nowhere near perfect." She waved her hand in frustration as hot tears fell down her cheeks. "All I am is a disappointment."

I grabbed her chin in my hand again. "Are you about done telling me how I see you?" I demanded, my tone harsher than I meant it to be. The pain reflecting in her eyes broke something in me. "Who said you're not good enough? I'll kill them," I said darkly.

"You can't just go around killing everyone, Tank," she protested as she threw her hands up in the air.

"Wanna bet?" I replied.

"That's beside the point. Leona needs me. I can't get distracted," Katrina said, her voice laced with desperation.

"She needs her mom to be happy, Katrina. Why can't you be happy?" I countered, trying to make her understand. Make her see what I saw when I looked at her.

"I don't deserve it!" she cried, her voice shaking.

"Why don't you deserve to be happy?" I murmured, my brows furrowed.

"Because I'm married, Tank. My parents married me off to the highest bidder. All I've ever been is a pawn, and I can't let that happen to my daughter. I just can't," she explained, her voice breaking with emotion.

I needed her to understand that she deserved to be happy, that she deserved to be loved.

"Look at me," I begged.

But still, she shook her head and refused to meet my eyes. Stalking across the room, I wrapped a towel around my waist.

Once I finally sat down beside her, I spoke softly, "Leona will never go through that, you hear me? The Dark Legion would never let that happen. *I* won't let that happen." But it wasn't enough to make her look at me.

"Me and Scar lost our sister, Rose, to the Hive. She was barely twenty when they took her. When she died...." I paused, emotions bubbling in my chest. Clearing my throat, I continued, "We dedicate ourselves to helping women and children involved in the skin trade."

Katrina's eyes flashed up to mine in surprise.

"We look out for ours. And when Scar saw you in that gas station, he knew you belonged here. *Both* of you."

"Tank, I'm sorry. I had no idea. I can't even imagine what that must have been like for you and Scar."

I shrugged, feeling a lump in my throat. "It was a long time ago. But it's why we built this MC. We look out for each other. We're family."

Katrina nodded, seeming to understand. "I want to believe you, Tank. I really do. But it's hard for me to trust anyone, let alone a group of bikers."

I could understand where she was coming from. The Dark Legion had a reputation, and it wasn't always a good one. But I knew we were different. We weren't a group of thugs riding around, causing havoc. We had a purpose, and that purpose was to protect those who couldn't protect themselves.

"Pretty girl, I know it's hard for you to trust us. But I promise you. We're not like the Hive. We have a code. We protect each other. And we will protect you and Leona, too."

Katrina was silent for a moment, then she reached out and touched my hand. "Tank, I...I don't know what to say. I'm scared. I'm scared for Leona. Scared for myself. But when I'm with you, I feel safe. For the first time in my life, I have hope."

I squeezed her hand gently. "There is hope, Katrina. There's always hope. And the MC will be here for you and Leona every step of the way."

"Why?" she asked, her eyes brimming with tears.

"Because you need us just as much as we need you. Because your daughter deserves a safe space to grow up. Surrounded by people who adore her and have and *will* kill to protect her. Because you deserve to be loved. Because I want you here. Pick any of those reasons. They're all true."

"Are you saying you love me, Tank?" she whispered, her voice filled with disbelief.

I tucked a strand of hair behind her ear, hoping my words wouldn't scare her away. "I've been falling for you since the moment we met. If I have to tell you that you're beautiful every day, I'll do it. Until one day you see yourself the way I see you. A woman who has been dealt a shit hand and does everything she can to survive in this fucked up world. A mother who will go to bat for her child and puts her daughter's wellbeing above all else."

A sob burst free from her throat, one she tried to muffle with her hand. I couldn't take the distance between us anymore. I pulled her into my chest. Her arms banded around my waist as she cried.

Once she finally calmed down, she leaned back and gave me a small grateful smile. I brushed the stray tear from her cheek and gently kissed her lips. I expected her to pull back, but then she rose up on her knees to deepen the kiss. Her hands tangled in my hair. I groaned. She tasted sweet and salty.

Delicious.

"Tank," she murmured against her lips.

"Lay down."

Katrina crawled up the bed and positioned herself on my pillow.

Damn*, even after crying, she still was beautiful.*

Letting go of the towel, I crawled up the bed. When I reached her parted legs, I ran my hands down her thighs, tracing along her smooth skin. Her scent sweetened, telling me she wanted me to go further, but I needed to hear it with words.

"Tell me what you want," I said huskily, still tracing small circles on the sensitive skin of her thighs.

Everything about her was soft against my calloused fingers. Katrina's breath caught when I inched higher. Her legs fell open, silently inviting me to explore her more.

"Do you want me to touch you, pretty girl?" I purred.

She nodded, and a sexy as fuck blush crept up her chest. I smirked.

She was nervous.

"Words, Katrina," I growled, leaning forward and placing a kiss on the inside of her knee.

"Yes," she breathed.

"Yes, you want me to touch you?" I asked again. She nodded.

I kissed and licked a trail down her inner thigh. Her soft gasps and moans—the sweetest sounds. I swirled my tongue along her breast's underside before biting down softly. Her fair skin turned red almost immediately. I groaned in satisfaction. My Cerberus loved how beautiful her skin marked for us.

My fingers found the hem of her shirt, but her hand shot out and gripped my wrist to stop me. My gaze flicked up to hers. The firm set of her jaw and the way her brows pinched made me hesitate.

"Are you hiding from me?" I asked softly.

"I told you, I'm not beautiful. I have scars and--"

A deep growl rumbled through my chest. "I don't care. I want to see you. All of you."

Slowly, her grip on my wrist loosened, but despite that, she wouldn't meet my gaze.

"Do you want me to stop?" I asked, brushing the hair from her face.

Her cheek pressed into my palm, a breath of relief fell past her lips. I would never force her. I would wait for her if she didn't want this to go any further.

"You tell me if you want to stop. You hear me?"

"Okay."

She nodded, a small smile on her lips. I gently kissed her lips, slowly lifting the hem of her shirt. When she didn't stop me, I kissed a trail down her neck to her breasts and squeezed them gently. Katrina wrapped her arms around her stomach. Her gaze moved to the wall behind me.

"Let me see you, pretty girl," I murmured.

With a shaky breath, her hand moved to grip the sheets at her side. I swirled my tongue around her nipple, earning me a soft moan. Pushing her shorts to the side, I teasingly ran my fingers down her slit.

Leaning back, my gaze roamed over her curves as I continued to swirl my fingers along her clit. Everything about her was sexy. The freckles that dusted along her collarbone. The soft swell of her stomach covered in tiny white scars and hips I couldn't wait to grip while I fucked her.

"Do you want more, pretty girl?"

"Tank," she moaned. A shiver ran down my spine, hearing my name on her lips.

Tugging down her shorts and panties, I took in her beautiful curves. Her breast bounced slightly with each breath. She arched her back, her legs quivering with anticipation. Her scent surrounded me. My cock throbbed, desperate to fill her.

Needing to feel more of her, my fingers dipped between her folds. Her walls clamped down like a vise, sucking me into her deeper. Her excitement made my fingers slick as I rubbed circles over the bundle of nerves. Her hip bucked slightly under my attention. I chuckled darkly.

So responsive.

I nibbled and sucked on any part of her I could reach. Marking her.

Mine.

"Fuck, baby. You're so damn tight," I growled. My molars

ground together as I flicked that spot deep inside her.

She tossed her head back, revealing the slender column of her throat. The beast in me wanted to collar her, feel her pulse pound against my palm as she climaxed. But she wasn't ready for that. Not yet.

Her skin flushed, a light sheen of sweat appeared along the swell of her breasts.

"Fucking beautiful," I praised.

I took my time exploring her pussy. Savoring every sound. Every scent. Every taste. I couldn't take it anymore.

I need more.

Katrina moaned in protest as I slipped from between her thighs. Her arousal glistened on my fingers in the dim light. I inhaled deeply, basking in her musky scent.

My mouth watered.

Hungrily, I plunged them into my mouth, tasting her for

the first time. Sweet and savory notes burst on my tongue. I groaned in pleasure. Her eyes widened as she watched me suck my digits clean.

I gripped her ass roughly, groaning as she spread her thighs as far as they could. With the flat of my tongue, I licked up her slit. She cried out in pleasure. Her body jerked and twitched as I circled her clit, again and again. I plunged two fingers deep inside her.

"Tank," she said, her voice hoarse.

Her thick thighs wrapped around me, heels digging into my back as she pulled me closer, taking her pleasures from me. I growled in approval. Her dainty fingers gripped my hair, nails digging into my scalp. The slight bite of pain spurred me on. My cock throbbed for release. With my free hand, I pinched her nipple and rolled it between my fingers. Katrina's cries grew louder.

"Come for me, pretty girl," I demanded, my voice barely audible.

I flicked my fingers faster, pumped them harder. Her walls spasmed around my fingers. The sounds of her slick pussy and moans filled the space around us.

With a sharp inhale, Katrina's body locked, and she threw her head back as she found her release. I licked her, tasting her cum.

Fuck, I could never get enough.

Her body slumped, and her chest heaved as she attempted to catch her breath. I wiped my mouth with the back of my hand and crawled up the bed to lie beside her. Her eyes flicked down to my still-hard cock, then back to mine.

"I'm fine, pretty girl. Tonight was about you." I opened my arms to her, content to simply hold her close.

Her head rested on my chest, and I had one arm tucked behind my head as I stared at the ceiling. I absentmindedly drew my fingers back and forth through her soft hair.

"Tank?" I hum in response. "That was my first."

My fingers stopped their movement as I took in her words.

That was her first orgasm?

"First of many, baby," I promised. "Try to get some sleep."

She nodded, burying her face deeper in the crook of my neck, and let out a soft breath.

Is she smelling me?

I smirked and kissed the top of her head with a content sigh of my own. I could still taste her on my tongue as I drifted off. She tasted like a slice of heaven. There was no way I'd ever get enough.

Chapter 15
KATRINA

I squeezed my thighs together as the memory of last night washed over me.

That tongue. That man and his damn tongue. I didn't expect it to feel that good.

Every experience I had with John paled in comparison. I cringed at the mere thought of my husband. Every sexual encounter with him was a tool for power. A punishment, a means for control. I was just too brainwashed to see it. Now that I had, I could only imagine all the things I'd missed out on.

My cheeks flushed. I tucked my chin and hid my blush with my hair, like a curtain shielding me from anyone who might notice the look on my face and guess all the dirty things I was thinking about.

I glanced over at the opposite side of the bar where Molly, Diamond, and Leona were having breakfast, completely oblivious to the night I shared with Tank. Leona threw her head back, laughing at something Diamond said. My chest warmed at the interaction.

Last night, Tank said the crew would look out for us. Look out for Leona, and I found myself believing him.

My eyes filtered around the room. Scar, Steele, and Nate sat at the table in the center of the room. Three chairs at their table sat empty. Tank said he was going to check in on Snake this morning, and my stomach twisted with nerves. I should have gone with him. My eyes landed on Scar. His normally cool persona was missing. My brows furrowed, and I gnawed my lower lip.

Should I go over there?

Scar's shoulders were tense, his gaze downcast on the table as he pushed food around with his fork. There was an ominous feeling wafting off their table.

What's wrong?

I stood up and shuffled across the room before realizing what I was doing.

"Everything okay?" I asked, shuffling from foot to foot.

Scar's honey eyes lifted to mine, softening slightly. "Morning, dove. Have a seat." His deep-velvety voice sent a shiver down my spine.

Collapsing into the chair next to Nate, I gave him a shy smile. We hadn't talked much since that day in the gym.

Steele placed a cup of coffee in front of me. A smile tugged on his lips. "To replace the one you left at the bar."

I murmured a thanks and took a sip. All three men began eating once again. Steele ran a hand down his face, a sigh escaping his lips. I shifted in my seat awkwardly.

"How's Snake?" I asked him, needing to fill the silence.

Steele's gray eyes met mine again. His brows pinched.

"He's a stubborn bastard. He'll be fine," Scar answered, shooting Steele a look I couldn't decipher.

Feeling bold, I lifted my chin and gave Scar a look of my own. He raised one brow in challenge.

Oh, it's on.

Never once breaking our stare off, I leaned closer, placing my elbows on the table, my chin in my hands.

"So, you're not going to tell me what's going on?"

Scar's lips ticked up into an amused smile.

"It's club business, dove." His tone told me it wasn't up for discussion.

Well, fuck that. I'm tired of living in the dark. I mean, I just found out that the supernatural existed! What else don't I know?

A whole hell of a lot, apparently.

Breaking our stare off, my eyes flicked to Nate, who wouldn't look up from his plate.

Club business?

"What does that even mean?" I grumbled.

Steele and Scar shared another look. Some silent conversion that I wasn't privy to. It was pissing me off. I don't know where my boldness was coming from, but I decided to embrace it.

I deserved answers.

"You claim I'm safe here. So give me something." I wasn't opposed to begging to get some answers. "Please."

Scar cleared his throat and stood. The chair scraped against the wooden floors as he rose to his feet.

"You want to know more about the club?" he asked, his head tilting slightly as he studied me. I nodded, my voice getting caught in my throat as I took all of him in.

Scar wasn't traditionally handsome. He was rugged, manly. His hair is an unruly mess, a thick beard covering half his scarred face. The same broad shoulders as Tank.

Tank.

I swallowed nervously.

How am I thinking about Scar, when I had just spent the night in his brother's bed?

"I want to show you something." Scar held out a hand for me to take.

The bird chirped in the distance as we walked. I couldn't stop myself from stealing glances of Scar as we trekked deeper into the bayou. After a few moments of silence, I couldn't take it anymore. My voice broke the silence.

"What happened to Rose?" I asked, my eyes fixed on the ground. I felt guilty for asking about something so personal, but after what little Tank told me about their sister, I needed to know more.

"She was twenty when she was sold to the Hive. Rose was carefree... So full of life. Shadow, my father, the president of Shadow Devil's MC, isn't a good man. He saw women as a meal ticket and a bargaining chip," Scar began.

"I had already moved out of my childhood home when Rose was born. Tank was barely ten. As the eldest sibling, I made it my responsibility to look after her. Keep her from my father's ruthless clutches. One I have experienced more times than I can count."

"Is that why you moved out?" I asked in horror.

"Yeah, I tried to take Tank with me. But his mother wouldn't allow it. Selfish bitch," he spat through clenched teeth. I could see the pain etched on his face. All I wanted at that moment was to take it all away.

"It's not your fault, Scar," I said, reaching out to touch his arm. Scar gave me a sad smile, one that didn't reach his eyes.

"Tank, as he got older, started to notice more and more of my father's dark and twisted ways. He took out his anger on

Tank, too..." Scar's voice trailed off for a moment, and he took a deep breath before continuing.

"There was only one I trusted with the safety of my sister. Reaper. He knew how cruel my father truly was. Reaper would take Rose when my father had one of his many episodes. Their bond grew over time, and slowly they fell in love. Young love," Scar scoffed bitterly. "My sister became pregnant, and my father was furious. He punished us all with his trade."

"Trade?" My gaze searched his, needing to understand. Scar collapsed on a fallen log, his elbows rested on his knees, and a faraway look crossed his rugged face.

"The Hive isn't just another MC, Katrina. They run the world's most influential skin trade. My father sold my sister to those bloodsuckers," he spat, finally turning to face me.

"I'm so sorry," I whispered, tears brimming in my eyes. Realization dawned on me. John had sold Leona to the Hive too.

"It's not your fault," he said, taking my hand in his. "It's why we created the Dark Legion MC. Reaper, Tank, and I created this brotherhood six years ago. We will do just about anything to take the Hive's organization down. But last night didn't go according to plan. The women we intended to rescue weren't even at the site we had been watching for the last few months. It's almost like... someone tipped them off," he added, his brows furrowed.

"That's how Snake got hurt?" I gasped.

Scar nodded. "He'll be fine. One of our prospects, Chris, stayed with him all night."

Chris? Where had I heard that name before?

"What about you, dove?" His question interrupted my thoughts. "You're quite the anomaly," Scar said, obviously trying to change the subject.

I blushed under Scar's intense stare.

"What about me?" I asked, feeling put on the spot.

"Who hurt you? And don't try to deny it. Snake told me

about the bruises." He raised a brow, daring me to deny it. It reminded me that Snake had found out.

How long ago was that now? A week.

I touched my rib tentatively. "M-my husband."

My gaze fell to his boots. Ashamed to admit it. Scar lifted my chin and forced our gazes to clash again.

"He's a dead man," Scar growled, his eyes flashing bright yellow. My stomach coiled at the promise in his voice. "Show me."

"Are you a Cerberus too?" I whispered, ignoring his demand.

"No. My siblings and I don't share the same mother. Each of us possesses a different beast. Now quit trying to avoid me. Show me, dove," his voice softened.

"There isn't anything to show. I'm fine."

Scar frowned. "Prove it."

I groaned. "You're not giving up, are you?" I asked.

A smile tugged at the corner of his lips.

Standing, I turned my back to him. My hand shook as I lifted my shirt and revealed my back, littered with scars. A deep and feral growl rumbled from Scar.

"What did he do to you?" he whispered, a tenderness in his voice that had tears in my eyes.

"Scar, please don't ask me," I begged.

Scar turned me to face him, my shirt falling back into place and once again concealing my scars. His eyes searched mine before he pulled me to his chest. For a moment we just stood there, soaking up the strength we offered each other.

"You should know, my brother isn't the only one who cares about you, dove. We all do." His voice rumbled against my chest. "You're family now, and we protect our own."

I nodded, feeling a lump form in my throat. "Thank you, Scar. I'm grateful for all of you." Offering what little comfort I could, I squeezed him tighter.

Chapter 16

TANK

"How you doing?" I asked Snake, who was propped up in bed with a plate of untouched food.

He flashed me a sad smile. "Been better."

Once again, guilt began to weigh on me. I turned to Doc, who was currently checking stats on a clipboard.

"How long until he can ride again?" I asked.

"A few weeks at least. As long as this one here remains a good patient," he said, hooking a finger in Snake's direction.

"Me? I'm an excellent patient, Doc," Snake said, feigning innocence.

Doc rolled his eyes and smiled fondly at him. It wasn't the

first time he had treated Snake for injuries, nor would it be the last. Doc had been with us since the very beginning, and he was someone I trusted. If anyone could help Snake, it was the older mage. His healing magic wasn't instantaneous, but the herbs he infused with magic definitely were remarkable.

"You're a horrible patient," Chris grumbled from a chair near the window. I chuckled. He wasn't wrong. Snake could hardly ever sit still.

"Would ya' rather be in the kitchen than sittin' with little old me?" Snake teased.

Chris' eyes widened comically. "No, man. I'd rather be here with you," he blurted, not wanting to offend Snake.

I smirked, knowing how my grams worked the prospects in her kitchen. She was old school like that.

"You better watch out, prospect. Snake might make you his personal nurse if you're not careful," I joked.

Snake laughed, and Doc shook his head at our banter.

It was moments like this that made me realize why I loved this brotherhood so much. We were a family, and we took care of each other.

I took a seat next to Snake's bed and studied him for a moment. He had a few bruises on his face and a bandage on his leg, evidence of the shit show of a failed mission that had taken him out of commission for a while. It was always tough seeing one of our own hurt, but it was part of the lifestyle we had chosen. We knew the risks, and we accepted them.

"You need anything, brother?" I asked, placing a hand on his shoulder.

"Nah, man. Just some rest," he said, his eyes closing for a moment before they opened again. "But if you could bring me a beer later, that'd be great."

I chuckled. "I'll see what I can do."

A few days ago I had pinky swore Leona and I would make a lei together. After last night's epic fail, I was content spending the afternoon in the garden, making necklaces. Much like Rose and I used to do.

As I watched Leona's delicate fingers thread the flowers onto the string, I stretched out on the blanket, shutting my eyes and basked in the afternoon rays. A sense of peace washed over me. Despite the chaos and violence that often surrounded Dark Legion, moments like this reminded me why I was doing it all.

For my family. For Rose.

My eyes scanned the garden.

Grams and Diamond were picking vegetables for my grandpa's world famous stew. One we still honor at the dinner table years after he's passed on.

Nate sat under a wide oak, his nose buried in a book. Wild red hair covered most of his face.

A group of teens sat at the picnic table, gossiping and laughing. I smiled. They reminded me so much of Scar and Reaper growing up.

The people who had chosen to stand by my side and built this life with me. My support system, my motivation to keep striving for a better tomorrow. Every decision we had made, every obstacle we had overcome, was to build this.

My gaze shifted to Leona, her dark hair shining in the sunlight as she bent over the necklace she was crafting. Looking up from her work, she gave me a smile, one that I returned. She truly was a ray of light in the darkness, unique and wise beyond her years. I could only assume it was because of the hardships life had thrown at her.

"What color beads are you going to use?" I asked, choosing a bright blue for myself. Ocean blue, like Katrina's eyes.

"Purple!" She grinned brightly.

I chuckled at her enthusiasm. The excitement was refreshing and infectious.

"How old are you Leona?" I asked, wanting to know more about her and her mother.

"I'm this many," she said, holding up her hand, and wiggled all five fingers.

I chuckled at her childish gesture and quickly high-fived her. Her laughter was like music to my ears, and I couldn't resist teasing her.

"Wow, you're so old already!"

"Am not! How old are you?" she asked, sticking out her tongue.

"36." I winked. "So, I get to decide what's considered old."

Leona giggled, and I felt a warmth spread through my chest. She was so pure and innocent, and being with her made me want to be a better man.

"Finished!" she announced, holding up her necklace triumphantly.

"The pink and white flowers were a good choice."

"Let me see yours," she demanded, making grabby hands at my lei. Chuckling, I handed her my necklace, feeling a little nervous about what she would think.

"I made it for your mama. Do you think she'll like it?" I asked tentatively, truly curious what she would think.

Leona's brows furrowed in concentration as she studied the white flowers surrounded by blue gems. One thing about children, they were brutally honest. I waited on bated breath for her answer.

"I think mama will love it." She beamed, handing it back. Sighing in relief, I chuckled nervously. "But I think mine is better."

"You little–" I laughed, reaching over and tickling her in retaliation.

The sound of a motorcycle's engine rumbled throughout the garden. I turned my head, my eyes following the source of the noise until I saw Reaper rounding the corner. He rode slowly, almost hesitantly, before coming to a stop. Without a word, he threw his helmet on the ground and stormed in my direction.

My heart skipped a beat as I noticed the dark circles under his eyes and the tension in his shoulders. He hadn't come back to the clubhouse last night, and I was worried about him. If anyone took last night's failure to heart, it was him. He never took death well. The burden he bore made sure of that.

The garden, which had been buzzing with life just moments ago, was quickly vacated by most of the club. Whenever Reaper was around, people scattered. Not that I blamed them. Reap was one scary motherfucker. I stood, waiting for him to say something, anything.

"Nice of you to finally come home, brother," I said, trying to keep my voice light.

He grunted in response, pulling at the worn leather gloves he always wore. My brows furrowed in concern. The only time he would seek me out like this was to spar. To help rid himself of all his inner demons. I wouldn't claim that it was the healthiest way to get through something, but I would never tell him no.

Before we could start, however, Leona appeared, tugging on Reaper's cut. I winced, knowing how much he hated being touched. But to my surprise, he didn't push her away. Both our gazes shifted to hers.

"When I'm sad, my mommy always does something to help me feel better," she said, holding out the necklace she had made. "Maybe this will help you."

For a moment, there was silence.

"Leona, why don't you go with grams and Diamond? I need to take care of something," I said, knowing Reaper was about to explode for touching him, and Leona didn't deserve that.

The rigid set of Reaper's jaw slowly relaxed, and his eyes darkened with emotion. It was as if Leona's small gesture had broken through the wall he had built around himself.

Without a word, he took the necklace from her and held it in his hand, staring at it as if it were the most precious thing in the world.

My shoulders sagged in relief, a lump forming in my throat at his sigh. It was rare to see him show any sort of vulnerability. But as I watched him standing there, holding onto that necklace like it was a lifeline, I knew that he was hurting in a way that words could never express. And in that moment, I felt a deep sense of gratitude towards Leona. For reminding us all that sometimes, the smallest things could make the biggest difference. She truly was just what my crew needed. She and her mother both.

I walked into the training room, my heart racing as I saw Tank already there, his muscles glistening with sweat. This wasn't the first time we had trained together, and I was getting better, more confident. Tank's eyes met mine, and I felt my breath catch in my throat.

Damn. He's always been able to make my heart skip a beat with just a look.

It's been three weeks. Three *long* weeks since that night we shared. I was going crazy. The sexual tension between us was growing every day.

I don't get it. Why hasn't he made a move?

I sighed in frustration and threw my hair in a messy braid, trying to focus on today's sparring session. But it was hard when he was so damn distracting.

"Morning," I said, strolling across the gym toward the ring.

I went through the motions, each move bringing Tank and me closer together. His touch sent shivers down my spine. The heat of his body set mine on fire. I felt a surge of desire every time his breath whispered against my skin. I tried to focus on the training, but it was getting harder by the minute.

Fine. Two can play that game.

I was determined to distract him just as much as he was me. I knew he could smell what he was doing to me. Every day here in the gym, my libido went crazy. Tank smirked.

Yup, he knows damn well what he's doing to me. Asshole.

The next time his arm encircled me from behind, I pushed back, shamelessly rubbing against his erection.

"What are you doing, pretty girl?" Tank breathed into my ear. I shivered. I meticulously rubbed against him further, my heart in overdrive.

Suddenly, Diamond walked in, interrupting us. She teased us with a grin, knowing full well what was going on between us. I felt a blush spread across my face, but I couldn't deny the electricity in the air.

"Morning Kat, Tank," she said, heading into the locker room.

We shared a look, my face flaming red.

We continued sparring, the tension between us growing with each passing moment. Tank's eyes roamed over my body, and I could feel the heat building between us. I knew I was using his attraction to me to distract him, but I was determined to pin him. I wasn't above playing dirty.

Finally, I got the upper hand and pinned him down. He looked up at me with a wicked grin, and I could feel the desire radiating off of him.

"You're getting better," he said breathlessly, his voice low and husky. "But you still have a long way to go."

I couldn't take it anymore. I grabbed his wrists and pinned

him down, straddling him as I held him in place. Our bodies pressed together, and I could feel his arousal against me. Our eyes locked, and I could see the desire burning in his gaze. I bit my lip, looking down at him as he grinned up at me, his hands coming up to rest on my hips. If I was a guy, I'd be thinking with the wrong head right now.

I leaned down and whispered in his ear, "I think I've learned enough for today. Don't you?"

He let out a low growl before flipping us over so he was on top of me. My stomach did somersaults. His body pressed against mine, his meaty fingers dug into my hips.

"Oh, I'm not done with you yet, pretty girl," he said, his voice husky with desire. "I want you so desperate for me you beg for it," he groaned.

I whimpered, ready to give in. I could feel my face flush at his words, and I knew that he could see the desire in my eyes, smell my pheromones in the air.

"Is that so?" I moaned, licking my lips. "What if I told you I already am desperate for you?" My heart beat in its cage.

I can't believe I just admitted that out loud.

He groaned, grinding into me harder. His feverish hands roamed over my body, sending shivers of pleasure in their wake. I moaned against his lips. A near kiss—just a hair's breadth from touching. My body hummed with pent up energy. Lifting my legs, I wrapped them around his waist. As I moved my hips against his, I could feel his arousal growing.

"Kiss me," I demanded.

"With pleasure," He growled.

Tank bridged the gap between us and pressed his lips against mine. Hot and feverish. Our tongues danced together, and I felt his hands grip my hips, pulling me closer to him. His lips moved down to my neck, nibbling and sucking on my skin, sending shivers down my spine. He pulled back and looked down at me as we both tried to catch our breath. His dark eyes clouded with a mixture of frustration and desire.

"You know what, Tank?" My voice is low, husky. "I think I am done with this training session."

The look in his eyes was like molten lava, swirls of red and orange. His Cerberus. A few weeks ago, seeing his beast would have scared me, but now it made me want him that much more.

Digging my heels into his back, I pulled him closer. I moaned softly, grinding my hips against him. "I want you," I said, my voice filled with desperation. "I want you so badly."

"Then take me," he growled, flipping us over so that he's below me once more.

His hands explored my body again, cupping my breasts through my tank top before sliding down to the waistband of my leggings. He pulled them down, leaving me in just my panties and tank top.

"You're so beautiful," he murmured, his eyes dark with desire. "I want to make you feel good, Katrina."

I arched my back into him. He pulled down my top, exposing my breasts. My nipples pebbled as he circled his tongue over the bud. His fingers traced patterns over my stomach before slipping under the fabric of my panties. His touch sent bolts of pleasure shooting through me, and I couldn't help but moan his name.

"Tank," I begged, writhing as his fingers curled inside me. "I need you."

And with that, he lowered his sweats, his cock springing free. I shed off my panties and centered myself over the ridge of his cock.

"God, Katrina," he groaned, his hands gripping my hips tightly, guiding me from below. "I want you too."

I took him in, inch by delicious inch. The stretch was exactly what I'd been craving.

"Fuck yeah. So tight, pretty girl."

His words sent a jolt of desire through me, and I moved faster, bouncing up and down on him with abandon. The sound of our skin slapping together filled the air, and I could feel myself getting closer and closer to the edge. As we moved together in a frenzy of passion, I knew that there was no going back from this. Tank and I were in this together, for better or for worse.

"Fuck, Tank," I moaned, my head thrown back in ecstasy. "I'm so close."

"Come for me, Katrina," he growled, thrusting up into me harder and harder. "Come on my cock, pretty girl."

His words pushed me over the edge, and I cried out as I came, my body convulsing in pleasure. I gasped as he ground his hips into mine, and the friction between us ignited a fire that I couldn't control. His hands found their way to my hips, holding me in place as he continued his slow, tantalizing movements, drawing out every ounce of my pleasure.

"Please," I whispered, my voice barely audible over the sound of our ragged breaths.

"What was that, pretty girl?" he asked, a smirk on his handsome face. His hair fanned out around his head. My pleasure began to build again.

"Fuck, Tank. I'm going to come again." I threw my head back, sweat dripped down my back. "Harder," I panted.

"Just remember you asked for it," he said darkly. The words sent a shiver down my spine.

Suddenly, he flipped us over, so he was on top of me. He stared down at me, his pupils blown. I arched my back, pressing myself against him, desperate for more.

He chuckled softly. "That's more like it. You look so beautiful when you come on my cock. Think you can handle another, my goddess?" he asked, his voice rough and raw. I nodded, unable to form words, my body trembling with anticipation. And then he took me, claiming me completely and utterly, his body moving in perfect sync with mine. "I've wanted you from the moment I laid eyes on you."

I moaned softly, the sound of his words sending another wave of pleasure through me. He leaned down, capturing my lips in a searing kiss. His tongue slid into my mouth, exploring every inch of me. I responded eagerly, my hands sliding up his back, pulling him closer to me.

The kiss deepened, becoming more urgent as our desire for each other grew. We were lost in each other, our bodies moved together in a rhythm that felt like it was always meant to be.

Tank growled low and deep, his gaze falling to my breasts that bounced with each thrust. His movements were fast and hard, his cock pulsing as he finished deep inside me. The hunger in his gaze pushed me over the edge. I cried out in ecstasy.

As we laid there, panting and trying to catch our breath, I knew that this was just the beginning. Tank and I had a long road ahead of us, but I was ready to face it all as long as he was by my side.

Tank groaned and turned toward me. "I wish we could lie here longer. But someone's coming."

Standing up on wobbly legs, I quickly dressed and peeked at Tank through my hair.

Within a few seconds of dressing, Diamond walked in, a smirk on her face. "Oh my god, are you two still at it? How many rounds have you gone today?"

I groaned in embarrassment, burying my face in Tank's chest. He chuckled.

"Don't even start, Diamond. We're just training."

She rolled her eyes at him and grinned. "Right, training. I'm sure that's all it is."

"Goodbye Diamond," Tank said, playfully.

Diamond held up her hands. "Okay, okay. I can see when I'm not wanted." She laughed. "Have fun, you two." She gave me a dramatic wink before heading out of the gym.

Once she was out of earshot, Tank and I shared a look. One that led to laughter bubbling up from my chest.

"I can't believe we almost got caught," I said, touching my lips. They felt swollen and sensitive.

"You wanna get out of here?" he asked, all traces of humor gone. A smoldering look pierced his eyes as he turned toward me. His chest heaved as he waited for my answer.

"Yes."

Chapter 18

TANK

I lounged back in my chair, watching wisps of smoke rise from the grill, and the savory aroma of sizzling burgers and hot dogs wafted over us. The sun beamed down on our backyard clubhouse, casting a warm glow over everything. It was moments like these, with good food and even better company, that made life feel complete. I lived for moments like this. The simplicity, and gathering with your loved ones. Food brings everyone together, and I loved being able to cook for my crew.

"Smells good," Katrina said.

Looking over my shoulder, I gave her a smile and clicked the tongs playfully at her. She laughed and swatted my arm. Her vanilla scent filled my nose. I inhaled greedily. Katrina fingered the hem of her shirt as she watched me.

"You doing okay?" I asked.

She nodded. "Just so many people." She scanned the yard that was bustling with people. "I've never really been around so many people at once."

I furrowed my brow in confusion. There was still so much about her that I didn't know.

"Why's that?"

"I was homeschooled growing up. Then, my parents arranged my marriage when I turned eighteen." She shrugged like it was no big deal.

I decided to ask about the safer topic. "Home schooled, huh?"

"Yeah, my parents owned a ranch on the outskirts of town. They only really went into town when getting supplies."

I flipped the burgers as I listened. But I wondered why they stayed so secluded.

"I'm starvin'," Snake said, coming up on my left as he clapped my shoulder.

"Nuh uh, you have to wait until everyone else can eat, too." Snake pouted, his lower lip stuck up as he batted his eyes at me. I laughed at his antics. "Your puppy dog eyes won't work on me."

"They'll work on my kitty Kat, though," he said, leaning his head on her shoulder.

"Just give him one hotdog," she said, patting his shaved head. "He's hurt."

Snake laughed. "See! She gets it."

"Fine." I pointed to the tin full of already cooked burgers and dogs. "But just one."

"Score!" Snake said, taking a huge bite. "Want some?" He dangled the hotdog in Katrina's face. She tentatively took a bite. I watched her lips as she chewed.

"Damn, kitty Kat," Snake purred. "Who knew I'd enjoy

watching you eat so much?" His voice turned husky. I smirked as the blush crept up her cheeks.

"Shut up," she said, smacking his arm.

"Ow! You hurt me."

Katrina's face turned serious. "How are you doing? Healing okay?" Her gaze shifted to mine. "Tank said you got hurt on your last run."

"Oh he did, did he? You all talkin' about me?"

Katrina frowned. "Seriously, are you okay?"

"You gonna be my nurse if I say no? Kiss my boo boo and make it better?" He wiggled his eyebrows suggestively.

"We give out kisses now, sweets? Where's mine?" Steele teased, pulling her into a hug. For a moment, she didn't hug him back, and I felt the need to step in. "Don't fight the hug, sweets. Embrace it." She giggled and wrapped her arms around his middle.

"So about that kiss?" Snake asked. Katrina's gaze shot to mine in panic, a question in her eyes.

"I can vouch. She does give the best kisses," I teased. I didn't want her feeling awkward and if she wanted to kiss someone else.

Who was I to stop her?

Katrina beckoned Snake over with a hook over her fingers. Grabbing him by the collar, she pulled him to her level. Steele and I waited on bated breath when she turned his face and kissed his cheek.

"That's all I get?"

"Oh, stop it, you big baby."

Katrina's smile took over her entire face. She truly was beautiful when she smiled. Her entire face lit up.

"Hey Kat," Diamond said, coming over to join the party. Apparently, I couldn't have Katrina for myself. Not that I really minded. There would be time for that later.

"Hey. Thanks for the clothes."

"Yeah, no problem. I kind of have a shopping addiction and I wasn't using any of it anyway." Diamond chuckled. "And I'm glad someone can put my addiction to good use."

Katrina laughed. "I appreciate it. These shorts are so comfy."

"And they look great on you, too," I chimed in.

Diamond smirked. "Easy there, don't get too flirty with my girl."

Katrina rolled her eyes. "Your girl? I think you're overstepping there, Diamond."

Diamond raised an eyebrow. "Oh really? You know you love me."

Katrina playfully shoved her.

I grinned, enjoying the banter between them. It was clear they had a close friendship, and I was happy for them. Even though there was a history between Diamond and the crew, I was glad she was finding her place and befriending Katrina.

"Listen up everyone!" Scar called out. "Food is ready and will be serve yourself. Grab a plate, there is plenty for everyone. Then take a seat at the table."

I filled my plate with delicious barbecue, feeling content as I took a seat at the table. Snake sat on Katrina's left, and I took the spot on her right. The warm sun beat down on us.

"Mama! Can I sit with Diamond and grams, please?" Leona said, rushing over to us.

"Yeah, that's fine, baby."

"Yay!"

She turned to take off, but Katrina yelled out, "Leona!"

She turned at the sound of her name and rushed back to give her mom a hug before darting off in the direction she came from.

Katrina watched her for a moment, her face softening. "She

really is happy here."

I hummed my agreement.

Scar stood up, holding up his beer to get everyone's attention. "Alright everyone, before we eat, I just wanted to take a moment to say something."

The chatter died down as everyone turned their attention to Scar. He took a deep breath.

"You know, when Reaper, Tank, and I started this club, we just wanted to ride together after we lost Rose." The club went silent as everyone took a drink in her memory. Scar cleared his throat. "But over the years, the club has become so much more than that."

He looked around at the faces of his family, his brothers and sisters. "We've created something special here. A place where we can come together as a community, where we can raise our kids and know they'll be safe, where we can take care of each other no matter what."

Scar's eyes fell on me, and he gave me a proud smile. "And I couldn't have done it without Tank's help. He's been there from the beginning, helping me build this brotherhood from the ground up. So cheers to you, brother."

The rest of the club raised their beers in a toast. I grinned and raised my own beer in response.

"But I also want to take a moment to recognize someone else. Someone who helped me create the Dark Legion and make it what it is today."

He walked over to grams, who was sitting at a nearby table, and put his hand on her shoulder. "Grams, you've been with us from the very beginning. You've seen us through thick and thin, and without you, we wouldn't be where we are today. You are the heart and soul of this club, and we all love you."

The rest of the club cheered and clapped, and Scar turned back to the group. "So let's eat, drink, and be merry, my friends. Here's to family, here's to community, and here's to the Dark Legion!"

A chorus of "To Dark Legion" echoed around the table.

"This burger is delicious," Katrina praised.

"Yeah man, thanks," Nate said from across the table.

"You're welcome." Tilting my chin down, I hid behind a curtain of hair. I loved taking care of my brothers, but I had never done well receiving praise.

"Yo Reap! Where have you been?" Snake called out. Reaper nodded in greeting and took the seat next to Nate.

"Let me get you a plate," Katrina said, hopping up from the table and dashing toward the grill. I knew she hadn't met him before, and Reaper was even more imposing than I was. He had this air around him that even the bravest men had run from him in fear. I sighed and got up from the table.

"Hey, you okay?" Katrina was placing a roll along with a burger on a plate.

"Fine." But her clipped tone and soured scent told me otherwise. Taking her shoulders, I turned her to face me.

"You don't have to hide from me, pretty girl. I know Reap can be a scary dude, trust me. But I promise you you're safe here, remember?" Her blue eyes lifted to mine, and she nodded.

"So come meet him. I promise he isn't as scary as he seems."

"Okay."

As we headed back toward the table, I placed a hand on her lower back. Something told me she needed my strength right now.

"Reaper, this is Katrina. Leona's mother," I said.

"Hi," she whispered, setting a plate before him.

"Thank you," he murmured. "Your daughter made me this." He pulled out the flower necklace that had begun to wilt.

"What the hell is that?" Snake said with a laugh. "Did you kill it already?"

"Shut up," Reaper growled. "It's a flower. It's bound to die, eventually." He shrugged like he didn't care either way, but I knew him. He did care. Leona was the first one to not cower in fear from him.

"It's lovely," Katrina said with a shy smile.

Snake leaned across the table. "Let me see it." Reaper narrowed his eyes at him, but did what he said. "Wanna see something cool, kitty Kat?"

He took Katrina's hand in his and laid the necklace on the table. With his hand hovering over the petals, he mumbled something under his breath. The flowers slowly revived, blooming fully.

"Wow! How did you do that?" Katrina asked in aww.

Snake shrugged. "Just a little jinn magic." His gaze shifted to Reaper. "Plus, I know this asshole loves them and this way they won't die on him. Since he kills everything he touches."

"Ha ha, very funny," Reaper said, reaching for the necklace and placing it on his neck. "Thanks, Snake." He grinned in reply.

I watched my crew eat and laugh together, and Katrina got more comfortable throughout the meal. And I'm reminded that there was no place I'd rather be.

Chapter 19.
KATRINA

Stepping out onto the porch, I inhaled deeply and the scent of pine calmed me. I couldn't remember the last time I had ever been happy. But a big part of me couldn't stop the doubt from creeping in. I had this nagging feeling something was about to go terribly wrong, even though I had no reason to believe it. There was always something being thrown at me, another curve ball that would uproot my life. I couldn't shake the feeling that something was going to happen.

"Mornin."

The sudden greeting made me jump. I hadn't realized I wasn't alone. My gaze landed on a familiar mop of blond hair and a bright smile. It was the same guy who wanted to take me on a tour of the clubhouse. The memory of Tank stepping in filtered through me, the date we shared. Our first kiss.

I forced myself to smile back.

"Morning." My skin prickled with awareness, and that uneasy feeling intensified. Something about this guy always felt... off. All I wanted to do was bolt.

"You don't remember me, do you?" he asked.

"Um." I quickly racked my brain for his name. "It's Chris, right?" I replied after an awkwardly long pause. The door behind me opened, saving me from this uncomfortable conversation.

A pair of dark brown boots stepped out onto the porch, and dark washed denim hugged strong thighs. A deep red shirt clung to well-defined abs. I swallowed, my throat suddenly dry. When my ogling became too obvious, he snickered. The sound traveled straight to my clit.

My gaze flicked up to his face, and a mischievous glint was in his piercing gray eyes. His crow perched on his left shoulder, its beady black eyes studied me.

"You got a little something…" His thumb ran over the corner of his mouth.

Oh. My. God. What is wrong with me? He just caught me checking him out. Is one dick not enough, Katrina?

Unconsciously, I wiped a hand across my mouth. Steele laughed, clearly enjoying my embarrassment.

"I was not drooling."

Even though this man was totally drool worthy. He didn't need to know that. My cheeks flushed crimson as I scowled at him, lifting my chin in defiance.

"Are you sure?" he teased. I narrowed my eyes, but said nothing. Steele lifted his hands in mock surrender. "Not that I mind, sweetheart," he whispered, his eyes tracing down my body dangerously.

Chris cleared his throat, drawing my attention back to him. "So, I believe I still owe you a tour?" he prompted, side-eyeing

Steele.

"Um, I'm sorry, Chris." My gaze flicked to Steele's. "I've got plans for the day, right, Steele?" I raised an eyebrow at him, silently pleading for his agreement. It was complete bullshit, and Steele knew it. A smirk crossed his lips as he slung an arm over my shoulders. I tried and failed to suppress the shudder that ran down my body at the contact. Cyrus squawked at the sudden movement, his wings fluttered to maintain balance. I eyed the bird warily.

"That's right, we're going into town today. Gotta pick up a few things," he told Chris easily. My shoulders sagged in relief as I watched Chris storm away. For a moment, I kinda felt bad for the guy, but just one thought of how slimy he was erased any trace of guilt I had.

Steele leaned in closer to me, his lips brushing against my ear. "You okay there, sweetheart?" he whispered, sending shivers down my spine.

I nodded, trying to ignore the way my body was reacting to

his. "Yeah, I'm fine." My voice was a little shaky.

Steele chuckled, his warm breath tickling my neck. "You sure about that?" he teased, his hand trailing down my arm. I pulled away, trying to hide the blush creeping up my neck.

"I'm sure," I said, avoiding his gaze.

Steele just grinned, obviously enjoying my discomfort. "Alright, well let's get going," he said, grabbing my hand and pulling me towards the stairs.

"What?" I said, pulling my hand free from his.

His easygoing smile was back and full of confidence. As if he didn't doubt that I would go with him. It was both intimidating and incredibly attractive.

"You and I are going to run errands. What? You didn't think I'd let you get away *that* easily, did you, sweetheart?" My stomach tightened at the sound of the nickname on his lips.

Damn him.

He was right to assume I wouldn't say no. But I couldn't let myself get too caught up in him. I had to remember that Tank was the one I was with, and I needed to stay faithful to him. As much as I enjoyed Steele's company, I couldn't let things go any further than they already had.

"Fine, but I need to go shopping." Men hated shopping, right? "It could take all day," I warned.

"Perfect," he purred. "We'll take my bike this afternoon. See you in a few, sweetheart."

As I waited for Steele to arrive, I shifted nervously on my feet, aware of the tension building between us. It was a mistake to agree to go with him, but Tank was too preoccupied with club business to accompany me. So, I found myself stuck with Steele and the uncertainty that came with him.

A wave of relief washed over me as I spotted Diamond across the yard. Perhaps she could join us and ease the awkwardness. I hurried over to her, hoping she would be interested in coming along.

"Diamond, what are you doing?" I called out.

She smiled. "Hey, Kat. Nothing much. What's up?"

"Steele and I are headed into town. I need to buy some clothes of my own." I pulled on the tightly fitted t-shirt. "Not that I don't appreciate you letting me wear your clothes," I added, not wanting to offend her.

She laughed. "I'd love to come along. I saw these super cute boots and I've been meaning to get a pair. Want to go to the mall?" she asked.

I nodded, relief loosening my tense shoulders.

As we waited, I leaned against the wall and took deep breaths to calm my nerves. Suddenly, Steele appeared with his trademark smirk, and my body tensed up.

"Hey there, sweets," he drawled as he approached us. "I see you brought a friend along. Didn't think you could handle being alone with me?"

Diamond rolled her eyes and linked arms with mine. "She doesn't need you, Steele," she quipped, her tone filled with amusement.

Steele chuckled darkly. "I can share, if she asks me nicely," he added, his eyes lingering on Diamond for a second too long. I felt a pang of jealousy, wondering if he was attracted to her. Absentmindedly, I climbed into the SUV and settled into the leather.

As we made our way to the stores, I tried to shake off my unease and focus on finding some new clothes. I never liked the way the clothing hugged my curves.

I ran a hand along a beautiful dark green cardigan, eyeing it longingly.

"You should get it," Steele murmured from behind me. Inhaling a sharp breath, I glanced over my shoulder.

His gray eyes intently focused on mine. I shook my head and continued browsing the plus size section. Why was it that all the clothes for heavy set women seemed to be made for a grandma? I eyed a pair of 'mom' jeans with a sigh.

How is anyone supposed to feel sexy in those?

"Hey, Katrina, how about this?"

Steele held up a neon pink tutu with a sly grin on his face. I rolled my eyes at his antics and rounded the next aisle. There he was again, wearing the pink tutu, and holding up a pair of hooker heels. A teasing smile appeared on his lips. He wiggled his eyebrows. I felt myself beginning to blush, but still I ignored him.

As we continued browsing the plus size section, Steele held up a funny hat with an enormous flower on it, grinning widely. "What about this?" he said, placing it on my head.

I let out a giggle at the ridiculousness of it and quickly took it off, handing it back to him.

"No way," I said, still laughing.

He shrugged, placing the hat on his own head. How was it, even in a goofy ass hat and bright pink tutu, he still looked handsome?

Steele then held up a pair of comically oversized glasses with a fake nose and mustache attached. "These are perfect for you," he said, grinning.

"No way." I laughed. Steele shrugged and added the glasses to his ensemble. "You look ridiculous," I said, pointing at his reflection in the mirror.

"I look like a movie star!" he exclaimed with mock offense, a hand on his chest.

Finally, I gave in and took the hat off his head and placed it on my own. He struck a pose in the mirror and encouraged me to do the same. With a deep breath, I followed his lead. I couldn't stop the bubble of laughter at how ridiculous we both looked, especially when Steele put on a fedora and struck another pose.

"What do you think?" he asked, winking at me.

I shook my head, still chuckling. "You're too much, Steele."

Finally, after several minutes of teasing and trying on funny items, Steele held up the same green cardigan. "Try it on," he encouraged, a cheeky grin on his face.

"Alright, alright, I'll try it on," I conceded, heading towards the fitting room with a smile on my face.

Steele chuckled. "Okay, okay. But seriously, you should try on this dress with it." He held up a body hugging black dress. "It would hug your curves in all the right places." His eyes darkened.

"Alright, I'll give it a go."

As I made my way to the fitting rooms, I could hear Steele's playful banter echoing behind me.

"Remember, Katrina, confidence is key! Own those curves like it's nobody's business!" he called out.

I laughed again. With his silliness, I did feel more confident and more at ease.. I tried on the dress and cardigan. I couldn't help but think how lucky I was to have a shopping buddy like Steele.

Barefoot, I exited the dressing room and saw Steele sitting in the only chair near a set of mirrors. In his hands was a simple pair of strappy heels.

"To complete the look." His eyes trailed down my curves. "Damn, sweetheart." His praise made my stomach tighten with anticipation.

Just then, I noticed Diamond standing in front of a full-length mirror, admiring her reflection.

She looked stunning in a black leather skirt and a midriff top that accentuated her flawless figure. My smile fell, my insecurities instantly returning. I was envious of her confidence.

"Wow, Katrina, you look gorgeous!" Diamond exclaimed.

"You too."

She grinned, adjusting herself again before heading back into her changing room.

Steele came up behind me, and his eyes met mine in the mirror. "Everything okay, sweetheart?"

"Fine," I answered.

Steele smiled at me warmly. "Don't worry, Katrina. I love your curves." He leaned in, placing his hands on my hips. "Gives me something more to squeeze." His hands gripped me harder.

I rolled my eyes. "You always know what to say to make a girl feel better," I teased.

Steele grinned at me. "That's because I'm the best shopping buddy in town. And don't you forget it!"

I couldn't help but laugh at his teasing, feeling grateful to have him by my side.

By the end of the day, my feet ached, but I was happy with the clothes I'd gotten. I couldn't wait to go back to the clubhouse.

"I had fun today," said Diamond.

"Yeah, me too," I admitted. I thought about Steele and how he was so goofy and fun. "We should head to the car, though. It's getting late."

Diamond nodded, and we headed toward the parking lot. I had this feeling someone was watching me.

Is it John?

My nerves had my hands shaking as I studied the mostly empty parking lot. My heart jumped into my throat as men suddenly surrounded us and blocked our path.

"What do you want?" I asked, trying to keep my voice

steady.

One of the men smirked. His eyes flicked over to me, a flash of red in their depths, before they settled on Diamond.

"We're just here to collect," he said in a menacing tone.

Dread pooled in my stomach as I quickly realized what was happening. They weren't here for me, but for her. I stepped in front of Diamond, my fists clenched at my sides. All of Tank's lessons filtered through my head.

"You're not taking her," I said, my voice shaking slightly as I took a fighting stance.

But the vampires were too quick. They grabbed Diamond and pulled her away from me, their claws dug into her flesh. I screamed out her name, but it was too late. They had taken her, and there was nothing I could do to stop them.

Steele rounded the corner, a knife in one hand. "Katrina, what happened?" he asked, pulling me into his warm embrace.

"They took her," I managed to get out.

"Who?"

"The vampires," I whispered. My eyes darted to the doorway of a nearby store, making sure no one overheard us.

Steele's gaze locked onto mine, a determined look on his face. "I should have never left you alone," he growled. "I need to get you back to the clubhouse."

"But what about Diamond? We have to save her," I said, my voice cracking. My heart raced with fear and adrenaline.

Steele's expression softened, and he gave my hand a reassuring squeeze. "We will, Katrina. But we need to regroup and come up with a plan first."

As we climbed into Steele's car and sped off, my mind raced with thoughts of Diamond.

Is she hurt? Scared?

I couldn't bear the thought of her being alone with those monsters.

Chapter 20
KATRINA

I paced restlessly in the empty clubhouse, the echoes of my footsteps a constant reminder of the absence of the crew. The weight of worry clung to me like a suffocating embrace and tugged at my insides with relentless force. I only hoped that Diamond would be okay once the club found her.

Unable to bear the silence any longer, I stumbled outside, hoping the night air would breathe some clarity into my racing thoughts. The crisp evening air sent a shiver down my spine. I wrapped my new cardigan around me tighter as I walked.

As I approached the garden, the moon cast a haunting glow over the deserted parking lot. As I ventured deeper into the garden, a chill danced along my spine, sending a wave of unease. My eyes darted around suspiciously. And then I saw

Chris, the prospect who had always unsettled me. A shadow seemed to cloak his figure, accentuating the darkness lurking beneath the surface.

I averted my gaze, instinctively trying to avoid the intensity of his stare. Something about Chris had always put me on edge, an unsettling aura that whispered danger. And now, with the club away, I felt vulnerable in his brooding presence.

Chris sat alone at the garden table, his features etched with bitterness and resentment. My steps faltered, hesitation flooding my veins as our eyes locked. In that moment, I could sense the depth of his animosity, a seething anger directed solely at me.

"You always thought you were better than me, didn't you?" Chris' voice dripped with hatred, each word like a venomous arrow aimed straight at my heart. I flinched, my steps falter-ing. "Rejecting me, acting as if I was beneath you, unworthy of your attention."

My heart skipped a beat, a mixture of shock and confusion

washing over me. I had never intended to belittle Chris or make him feel insignificant, but the rejection of his advances had clearly left a bitter mark on his soul.

The weight of his words bore down on me, filling the air with tension. I struggled to find my voice, afraid to anger him further. What was once a subtle discomfort between us had now transformed into an open wound. I had the sudden urge to flee, but I stood my ground.

But before I could respond, a second figure emerged from the shadows. I gasped in a mixture of surprise and relief.

Diamond. *How? Did she escape? Did the club rescue her?*

I hadn't heard the sound of the bikes returning. I rushed forward with relief flooding through me.

"Diamond!" I gasped, my voice catching in my throat. "How did you...?"

My words trailed off as Diamond's expression hardened, a malicious smile playing upon her beautiful face. I stumbled backward, my heart pounding with a mix of disbelief and unease.

"You thought you could just waltz in here and take what's mine?" Diamond's voice dripped with icy disdain, and her bitter laughter echoed through the garden. "Oh, Kat, you truly are blind."

Diamond stepped forward, her movements fluid and graceful, predatory. Her eyes locked with mine, an icy determination in their depths.

Confusion and betrayal clashed within me, leaving me disoriented and vulnerable. Diamond had been my friend, or so I had believed.

I struggled to make sense of the situation, my mind grasping for answers amidst the chaos. It left me with nothing but shards of shattered trust. My heart ached at her betrayal.

I was so damn tired of the secrets and lies.

My gaze darted to Chris, his eyes darkened with malice. Amid my swirling emotions, the wickedness that enveloped Chris and Diamond seemed to intensify in the shadows that danced around us.

I braced myself for a fight, determined to hold my ground. Deciding to strike first, I launched a punch towards her jaw. My fist connected with her face, a glimmer of satisfaction flickering within me. But that satisfaction quickly faded when a manic look crossed Diamond's pretty face.

Blood stained her teeth, and an evil smile pulled at her lips. A mix of fear and confusion washed over me, making it difficult to concentrate. Taking a shaking breath, I lunged forward once again, hoping to land another blow.

But Diamond's speed was unfathomable. She moved with such incredible swiftness that it was as if she disappeared and reappeared behind me in a blur of colors. Disoriented and caught off guard, a sharp pain tore through my shoulder, causing me to cry out.

The pain was sharp and immediate as Diamond's teeth sank

into my shoulder. I gasped, feeling the searing agony radiate through my body. It was then that everything clicked into place.

How have I not seen the signs? How has she managed to hide this secret from us all this time?

Vampire.

I screamed in rage. The wind carried my pain and horror into the night. Chris laughed sadistically as Diamond gained the upper hand. Terror seeped into my bones, rattling my very core. I desperately yanked myself free from Diamond's grasp. Agony radiating down my shoulder. My mind raced to formulate a plan. I fought with every ounce of strength I possessed, throwing punches and kicks, but it was futile.

"You should have never come here, Katrina." Diamond shook her head as she circled me.

I felt like prey as her eyes zeroed in on my throat. The blood from her bite dripped down my neck and soaked my T-shirt. Within a blink, she lunged for me again.

Diamond's strength was overwhelming, overpowering my attempts to defend myself. Each blow I landed seemed to have little effect, and frustration swelled within me. Fatigue made my movements slow and useless. Despite my best efforts, the realization sank in: Diamond was too strong, too skilled. The odds were stacked against me. But even in the face of certain defeat, I refused to surrender.

How can I compete with her supernatural abilities?

It was a losing battle, and deep down, I knew it. But still, I fought on, drawing upon every ounce of determination within me. Each swing of my fist and kick aimed at her felt like an act of defiance, a small rebellion against the overwhelming power she possessed. But as the seconds ticked by, victory was an impossible dream.

Diamond's unyielding strength prevailed, and my body ached with exhaustion. The fight had taken its toll, physically and emotionally. Yet, in the depths of my spirit, a flicker of re-silience remained a refusal to surrender to the darkness that threatened to consume me.

Diamond laughed. "Is that really all you got? Pathetic."

She lunged at me, her teeth latching onto my neck. Gritting my teeth to stop myself from crying out, I fought against the pain. I struggled to break free from Diamond's iron grip. My muscles strained against her supernatural strength. But she held me with unnerving ease, relishing in my blood.

As I struggled, my gaze turned to Chris, who remained seated, his eyes fixed on the chaos unfolding.

"You should have given me a chance, Katrina. Now, you'll finally get what's owed to you."

Defiance welled up within me, fueled by the pain and the overwhelming sense of betrayal. I refused to be a victim of their wicked games. I launched myself forward with renewed determination, aiming a series of strikes at Diamond. But she effortlessly dodged and countered every move, her speed and agility surpassing anything I had imagined.

Chris' laughter echoed through the garden, fueling my anger and frustration. Every blow I landed seemed to have little effect, and the realization of my powerlessness gnawed at my spirit.

How could I have underestimated Diamond and the depths of her abilities?

But just when hope seemed lost, a figure emerged from the shadows, commanding all of our attention with their presence. I could feel their gaze upon us, assessing the situation. Recognition flickered in their eyes as they locked onto mine, a connection that sent me a fresh wave of ice-cold fear.

The garden fell silent, the tension thick in the air. I held my breath, waiting for him to make a move. Fatigue and blood loss sent me down to my knees, the gravel digging into my skin. Tears of defeat ran down my face. At that moment, fate caught up with me. This figure standing before us would be my downfall.

Epilogue
SNAKE

As we raced towards the Hive's hideout, my heart was pounding with anticipation. Our mission was clear. We had to stop Venom at all costs. He was a dangerous enemy who always stayed one step ahead of us. We couldn't let him get away with his latest scheme.

But then Tank's voice broke through my thoughts, "Snake, something's not right." I could hear the unease in his tone.

"What do you mean?" I asked, feeling a sense of foreboding.

"I can't smell her," Tank growled in frustration. "Her scent isn't here."

Steele chimed in. "Let me send Cyrus ahead. He has sharper senses and can find her."

We all agreed, and we watched as Steele's crow flew ahead.

As we entered the hideout, the silence was deafening. It was like the Hive members had disappeared into thin air. But then we heard a faint humming sound in the distance.

Suddenly, we were attacked by a group of vampires armed with swords and knives. We fought back with all our might, refusing to back down even when outnumbered. Scar breathed fire, Tank used his brute strength, and I relied on my agility.

As the last of the Hive members fell, we caught our breath and looked around the room. But Diamond was nowhere to be seen.

"What the hell is going on here?" I muttered, scanning the room for any clues.

And then I saw it. Reaper's flower necklace had wilted. My heart sank. Something was seriously wrong with Katrina.

"Guys," I said, pointing to the necklace.

Reaper turned to me, his expression accusing. "What did you do?" he demanded, clenching the necklace in his gloved hand.

Realizing I had to explain, I took a deep breath. "I connected the necklace to her. If she gets hurt, the flower-"

My voice caught in my throat, and Scar punched the wall in frustration. Venom had taken our friends, and we were running out of time.

Suddenly, Steele's crow Cyrus flew back, squawking urgently. "Diamond's not here."

My heart sank even further. We had failed. Venom had out-smarted us again. My rage and fear boiled over. Venom had gone too far, and he would pay for it all.

"We have to find them," I said, my voice shaking with fury. "We have to save them."

Scar nodded, his eyes blazing with determination. "We'll tear this whole city apart if we have to."

Tank growled. "No one messes with our family."

I knew we were in for the fight of our lives. But we were a team, and we had each other's backs. As we made our way towards the hideout, I couldn't shake off the feeling of unease that had settled in the pit of my stomach. We had to find Diamond and Katrina and put a stop to Venom's twisted plans.

We screeched to a stop in front of the clubhouse, our bikes kicking up dust and debris. The sight that greeted us was one of utter devastation. Someone had smashed the windows to pieces, and the door was barely clinging to its hinges.

Chris emerged from the shadows, his clothes stained with blood. We rushed towards him, fear and dread rising in my throat.

"What happened? Where's Katrina?" Scar demanded, his voice shaking with anxiety.

Chris hesitated for a moment, his eyes darting between the members of the Dark Legion MC. Finally, he spoke, his voice barely above a whisper, "They took her. The Hive."

Tank's hands clenched into fists, his muscles bulging with rage. Scar let out a low growl, flames flickering in his eyes. Cyrus cawed menacingly.

My heart was pounding with a mixture of unease and guilt. We failed to protect them both, and now Katrina was in the hands of their deadliest foes.

"We have to get her back," I said, my voice low and determined.

Steele spoke up, his voice laced with concern. "But how do we find her? The Hive could be anywhere."

"We'll figure it out. From now on, we tell no one outside the immediate crew about our plans. We definitely have a mole among us," Scar replied.

He's right, but who?

My mind was already racing with possible leads.

Reaper's expression was unreadable, but his grip on the wilted flower necklace tightened. I knew what was at stake. His gaze connected with mine and a determined look crossed his face. He was ready to do whatever it took to get them back.

But then I spotted something splattered on the wall.

"Scar," I said in warning, walking closer. It was unmistakably blood.

"I told you I always win, Scar."

My blood boiled with rage. We had to act fast if we were going to save our friends.

"What do we do now?" Steele asked, his voice laced with concern.

"We find them," I growled, my voice low and dangerous. "No matter what it takes."

We locked eyes, a silent understanding passing between us. We hopped back on our bikes and revved the engines, tearing off into the night.

One thing is for certain, the Dark Legion MC was on the hunt for revenge, and we would stop at nothing for vengeance.

Instagram> @missrenaeauthor

Start reading:

Blood Moon Bonds Trilogy or The Gemini Duet on KU

Made in the USA
Las Vegas, NV
10 July 2023

74444595R00178